The Ten

An Anthology of New Writing

from The Writing Coach

Nightingale
Editions

First published in 2024 by Nightingale Editions
An imprint of Blackbird Digital Books
www.nightingale-editions.com

A CIP catalogue record for this book is available from the British Library
ISBN No 978-1-0686505-3-6
Cover design by Charlotte Mouncey at Bookstyle

Printed and bound in Great Britain by Clays Ltd, Elcograf.

Contents

Introduction
by Jacqui Lofthouse

Way back in 1992, when I enrolled in the MA in Creative Writing at UEA under Sir Malcolm Bradbury and Rose Tremain, we students were told, by Malcolm himself, 'This year, you are writers.' I still remember the impact those words had on me as a new writer with only a rough, half-finished novel to my name. *Really? Was this even possible?* Surely, I thought, if the great man himself had said it, it must be true.

And so, I went about my year of study in East Anglia with a sense of purpose and a new belief in what was possible for me to achieve. What I wrote, I told myself, mattered. That year, we were incredibly fortunate to have guest lectures from writers at the height of their careers: Iris Murdoch; William Golding; John Fowles and Susan Sontag. In addition, at the end of the year, those studying on the publishing module also produced an anthology of our work called *Mafia*. We also met a few influential literary types at a party at Malcolm's house and on the request of one bold student, one of them wrote down a list of recommended literary agents. As a group, we twisted that student's arm and insisted that the list was photocopied. I wrote to most of them and was lucky enough to subsequently land not only a contract with an agent, but also a deal with Hamish Hamilton and Penguin for my first novel *The Temple of Hymen*.

Since those days, I have gone on to have four novels published and to found a mentoring and development organisation for writers, *The Writing Coach*. It has been my honour to work with many writers who have made a great success of their writing careers. At *The Writing Coach* we work with our writers on mindset, craft and connection, both with their fellow writers, with readers and the industry. Recently, we began making connections with literary agents on behalf of our writers – and last year, the idea of an anthology began to form in my head.

I like to speak about how the 'first mystery' of a book (Tremain's phrase) is a rather miraculous thing. I believe there is something magical about the process by which our imagination conjures ideas. I often speak of alchemy. So it was that the idea for this project formed.

The Ten. The idea drifted into my head late one evening as I strolled over the Hungerford Bridge across the Thames. *The Ten.* Ten writers, I thought. Only ten. Ten months. Ten novels. And then, of course, ten agents.

So, it was born. I knew immediately that *The Ten* would be published by my imprint Nightingale Editions. What I did not guess was how thrilling it would be to see those writers develop, during the course of ten months, into a community of people with a shared passion and a shared goal. The idea of the book, I believe, carried each of them to a new level of seriousness with their writing. With this end point in mind, it became easier to show up at the page, even in the midst of a busy week. I believe that the promise – 'you will be published' – enabled the writers to visualise the outcome. The thrill of their words in print. But more than that. The knowledge that they were indeed writers. Their stories mattered. There would be interested agents – in a literary world which can often seem alienating. There would be readers, leaning into their worlds, finding moments of escape, of truth, of shock, of recognition.

Here, in the fictive spell conjured by our authors, we have nine novel extracts and one work of poetic memoir. Whether you love historical fiction, fantasy, Young Adult fiction, literary fiction, psychological thrillers, or the raw truth of memory, you will find something to entice you.

I am so proud of each writer who has contributed to *The Ten* – and I feel certain that this is only the beginning of ten varied and fascinating writing careers…

Jacqui Lofthouse, September 2024

No Place for a Young Woman
by Farhana Shaikh

Preparation

When Ayesha Shah was born, her mother cried for forty days and forty nights. She cried while nursing her, while performing her ablutions, while reciting her prayers. 'We're ruined, we're ruined,' she wailed. Day after day. Night after night.

Ayesha heard the story of her birth so many times as a child, it was imprinted on her mind like a dream. Imagined and reimagined. She could picture the scene as if it was a story she'd read. She tried to work out which bits were real and which bits were made up, but realised she would never know the truth. Not really. Not that it mattered, because the truth wasn't as much fun as fiction. That's why she loved books. You didn't need to work out if someone was lying.

Papa told it best. How he soothed her back to sleep, gently rocking the crib from side to side, telling her many a tale.

Shona, unsure but right next door, didn't sleep for weeks. Mama's screams kept her up for much of the night. She tossed and turned. Prayed the baby would settle, the mornings would bring better news. But Mama was adamant Ayesha's dark skin and thick frizzy hair was a bad omen. They were cursed!

Shona sighed, worried that she misspoke. Said too much. Maybe, she had it all wrong. It was such a long time ago now. Her old memories, even the happy ones, were fading. 'The mind has a habit of playing tricks on you,' she said.

Mama insisted her version was the only one that was true, and the others were false because they didn't even tell it from the beginning. When she was nothing more than a seed. According to Mama, she had done everything right in her second pregnancy. Reciting the verses, following doctor's orders: feet up, no chicken, no fish. She had even given up sugar! And it was going so well. The sickness was passing.

And then something happened around four months in, once the heat arrived. The long summer nights were endless. Mama's swollen feet couldn't carry the weight any longer. All the baby did was kick, kick, kick. Mama rubbed her tummy, told herself that boys kick. That's what they do. Especially when they are going to grow up to be strong. And she wanted her baby boy to be strong.

So, can you imagine her shock when the nurse told her it was a girl? She couldn't believe it. Refused to believe it. And then Ayesha didn't take to the breast. Not like the first time. Not like Khadija. Her eldest was so good, so perfect! But, this second child, this daughter, wriggled and screamed. It was no surprise the milk dried up. They had to feed her tiny body spoonfuls of honey for three whole days! See now. Such fuss, right from the very beginning.

Mama's story didn't stop there. She went one step further, added an afterword. Blamed Ayesha for everything, even what happened next. As if she was a magician who had the power to tamper with her tubes so Maryam and Choti were born girls too. And now there were four of them. Did she not realise just how much trouble she'd caused? Silly girl! What would people say about them?

The people! What people?

Mama dismissed her question with a glare. *The people down there, Ayesha. Do you never listen?*

They played a role in her life, and she needed to play along too. Otherwise, she would fall. And to fall would be to fail. She couldn't afford to fail. Not when there were four of them.

Chapter One

It was in the dusty air of the bazaar that the townspeople gathered. They had come to realise that nothing much happened in these parts but had come to accept Nahinpur for what it was: as dull a place as any. The town was landlocked: neither big nor small, neither north nor south, tucked somewhere in between like the dust that settled in the back alleys, largely invisible but a nuisance nonetheless. It was the sort of place that saw frequent visitors – the majority of whom didn't stay very long at all.

The Shahs lived in a two-storey building on the main road in and out of town. The houses were packed closely together, so much so that when an argument broke out, which it often did, the residents of the adjoining property could hear what was being said, word for word. Very few owned a television and most had no need for such a device; other people's business was entertainment enough.

If you sat by the window or on the balcony to read as often as Ayesha did, you could imagine the lives other people led. It was as if the stage was set, a picture was being shot and the director was moving everybody around, this way and that, responsible for their every move, their every expression.

By mid-morning the bazaar was bustling. Market stalls were bursting with ripe mangoes, and overgrown custard apples; okra and dhaniya impregnated the damp morning air. Men with their heads stuck in giant stainless-steel pots stirred curries with giant ladles. Mile-long rows of street food: vegetable korma, chickpeas, five kinds of dhal, lamb karahi, biryani, and nihari which had been slow-cooked all night, tempted hungry visitors.

The place was full of noisy exchanges, voices crowding on top of each other. There was the bartering between buyer and seller: 'Picked today, fresh, ten for one rupee, for you only.' The buyer was rarely willing to pay the seller what he wanted, especially for something as ordinary and in good supply as carrots: 'No, not too fresh, twenty for one rupee. What do you take me for? A fool?' The very mention of any price would rile the seller, for it would be much too low, half-half was fair, surely? But nevertheless, he would consider the offer: 'Take eleven but don't rob me further, I have a family to feed.' Hands in pockets, the buyer would turn up his nose and pretend to drift elsewhere, his eyes surveying the stock of the neighbour's stall. The seller would go off too, attending to more important business, fiddling with coins, or assessing his handsome stock before coming back and agreeing: 'Final price, sixteen for one rupee.' And then on the shaking of the hand or a tap on the shoulder, they would smile as if they had both come out winning. As if such a thing was possible. The buyer would pick up his goods and take leave, waving at his new friend with a parting shot that he would send his wife if he'd been cheated, for she always knew better than him.

There were other exchanges that were just as important. They had no monetary value, no cash was involved and yet, those perfecting the art went about their business in the same way, as if their lives depended upon it. The commodity here was information of any sort: news, gossip, rumour, scandal. Facts were not important. The truth, less so.

People were always talking; they often said too much when really they ought to know better, and word got around fast. A rumour whispered in the corner of the bazaar would find itself along the rooftops within minutes, such was the fervour for gossip in the surrounding area. Imtiyaz Shah, Ayesha's beloved father, warned his wife about her trivial pursuits, of giving her opinion on things which didn't concern her. But Zubeida relented – life for a woman was difficult enough without being told how to find her amusements.

Every morning, Zubeida set out early to visit the bazaar under the pretext of buying the freshest vegetables money could buy. The family only ate meat once a week. It was expensive and took too long to prepare. Vegetables were reliable and easy to work with. She could cook them while she prepared the chapatis.

'Be good,' she said, shooing her daughters away from the window.

Choti sulked, demanding that she be taken out too.

'Girls aren't allowed out until they are ripe,' Maryam reminded her.

Choti shrugged her shoulders to express her disappointment. Ayesha didn't mind it so much. Life out there seemed all hushed and rushed. With Mama away, she could read uninterrupted.

The four sisters sat in the living room waiting for their mother to return. There was no way of knowing how long she would be when she was out. Sometimes it was as short as ten minutes or as long as a few hours, and Mama never indicated which it would be. She always left them with plenty to do, warning them that Satan found work for idle hands. Once they had finished their morning chores – sweeping the floors and hanging the clothes out to dry – the girls sat by the fire. It had been a cold winter and they'd decided to make a quilt. Or rather had been directed to by their mother. She said the quilt would give them a chance to work on something together and be a keepsake for her to treasure as they would soon all be married.

Mama had been dropping hints like that for weeks now while helping them collect scraps of fabric, showing them stitches, techniques, how to tie knots and work the thread. There was a methodical approach to her instruction that spoiled some of the fun, leaving Ayesha feeling overwhelmed.

She watched her sisters closely as they selected their fabrics, cut them into shapes and began working on a design of their own choice. Khadijah stuck to tradition, focusing her efforts on a Mughal design inspired by a painting. Maryam insisted hers would be Islamic to please her Maker, and Choti wanted something pink and gold, fit for Bollywood royalty. It was surprising Mama had given them a choice at all. That wasn't like her. She much preferred to make decisions for them.

Pulling thread through fabric, making sure it didn't end up in knots, was hard work. Why did the stitches never look as good as Mama's? To do something just to please others was such a chore! Ayesha wished her sisters could see the task for what it really was; a covert method to begin what, according to Mama, was a long overdue conversation. Even so, in the quiet rhythm of stitching she realised she didn't want to displease Mama. Not *really*. To go against her would be sacrilege. So she did her best to put her mind to capturing her love of peacocks.

There was a certain power to stitching. As she worked the thread she could see Mama's face in her fabrics, full of disappointment. Lines where there were no lines just months ago. Mama was always tired these days, finding fault with the smallest of things: how she swept the kitchen floor or put the dishes away. There was some reason to complain about this, that, and nothing at all. No matter how much progress they seemed to make with the quilt, it was never quite enough.

It had started with the royal visit, hadn't it? As if the snake charmer had cast his spell on more than just the crowds as they waited for the Queen's arrival. Mama's moods took on a life of their own. And the hints that they were older, that they needed to take on some responsibility had begun right after Eid. Around the same time, Mr and Mrs Pathan announced that their daughter was settling in the foreign; marrying the handsomest, cleverest man that had ever existed! It was all Mama could talk about for an entire week.

Ayesha didn't realise then that things were only going to get worse because the Pathans had somehow – astagfirullah – forgotten to send the Shahs an invitation to the wedding. Despite lengthy explanations and apologies of an oversight, a small mistake, in the mayhem that weddings bring, the damage was done. Mama was furious. To not receive an invitation to the wedding was an insult. But to find out from Meena – of all people – that the Faisals had been to the walima was a number one humiliation.

Ayesha could hear Mama's voice in her head telling her to forget all that nonsense now and focus on what was right in front of her, to *make haste, girl*, because time was not on their side. It seemed it never was. Maybe if Mama wasn't always chasing time, it would be kinder to them all. Maybe then they would be able to make some progress at last. Her frequent reminders had the opposite effect, putting them into reverse mode. Even today, it didn't take them long to throw down their fabrics, abandon their needles, and look for something else to do.

The bare room was invitation for mischief. A single lamp sat on a pair of nested tables in one corner, and a wooden chair faced a sewing table in the other. A tall gold mirror hung from above the fireplace. Beside the settee, an old mahogany cabinet rested against the full width of the wall, as if it were supporting it.

The cabinet housed most of the family's possessions, the majority of which belonged to Mama: cups and saucers from Saudi Arabia; a miniature golden set of table and chairs; two picture frames, one of the Kaaba, the other of the Babri Masjid; a vase, and on the highest shelf sat an encrusted purple velvet box which housed the Quran. There were other books hidden out of view but not out of reach. Books that Papa had bought; Shona had gifted. Mama didn't understand. She believed nothing good ever came from books. But Ayesha didn't care. It was a different feeling when you were reading. It was magic.

Now and again, and always just before the rainy season, Papa would take them to Glasses Chacha's bookstore to buy a book each. That wasn't his real name, but it was the only one Choti called him when she was little, and the name stuck.

Mama complained, said it was typical of Papa to push *her* daughters further away. As if the comprehension of another language made them distant relatives.

Ayesha took up the opportunity to read when Mama was out because she frowned upon it, dismissing it as nothing more than a useless time-pass. She tried her best not to let that bother her, knowing it was the only time she was able to relax. She longed to spend the entire season reading without complaint. Just imagine how many books she could finish. Surely this marriage business could wait?

'This book doesn't make any sense,' Choti said, rubbing fatigue from her eyes after reading for just five minutes.

The four sisters were sitting on a single settee. All but one looked up to offer sympathy.

'Just keep going. You'll be fine,' Khadijah, the eldest, encouraged. She was a kind soul who was perhaps too gentle for her own good.

'What's happening in yours?' Choti yawned.

'If you give up already, you'll never work it out. I'd rather read something more important,' said Maryam, who cared neither for fiction nor fantasy.

'You know what happens if you read too much, don't you?' Choti said, making circles with her fingers and placing them over her eyes.

'I think they make him look learned,' Ayesha said, knowing exactly what Choti was doing without looking up. She was desperate to get to the end of the chapter before Mama came home.

'You would,' Choti said, undoing her plaits. 'A hero never wears glasses.' As the youngest she was considered a vain, feeble sort, but harmless all the same.

'Not everything is about looks, Choti!' Khadija scolded.

Choti replied with a shrug.

'Mama says reading is a terrible habit,' Maryam said. 'Nothing more than a trivial pursuit.'

Choti, who was considered too young to have an opinion, nodded.

'You're quite right, Maryam,' Ayesha said, slamming her book shut. She knew it was better not to say anything but the harder she tried to drown out her sister's bakwas, the louder it became. It was no good. As the person who

15

had taught them to read, she felt slighted. 'There are far more important things to do than waste time with books. We must train our minds, be beautiful and preserve our youth. We must learn to be passive, train our tongues to never speak out of turn. We must learn to cook simple dishes for everyday and complex dishes for banquets, for our husbands would starve to death if we didn't.'

'Fiction is just made up,' Maryam said, crossing her arms.

'I agree,' Ayesha replied. 'If we use our imaginations we'll get ideas above our station, make trouble for ourselves.'

'Come now. This talk is unbecoming of you both,' Khadija said, offering a hand to both. As the eldest, the role of peacemaker fell to her.

'Of course, we mustn't read,' Ayesha continued, ignoring the offer of reconciliation. 'We mustn't think too much either. Mama says thoughts are dangerous. Ideas could lead to a catastrophe.'

'Quick, she's coming!' Choti cried, as she paced up and down the room, desperately trying to re-plait her hair as fast as she could. 'I think I heard the door slam.'

'Pass me the books,' Ayesha said, snatching them out of her sisters' hands and shoving them under the settee.

They could hear Mama's footsteps and shouting as she made her way up the stairs and towards the living room. Her voice was rising, more agitated with every step.

The Boy Who Fell
by Gavin Marshall

The boy fell. Through a haze of white, a cold wind lashed his lungs. Down and down, deeper and deeper, he fell.

And fell.

And fell.

White haze became white sky. White sky became white foam as the sea, approaching fast, caught sight of the boy and pulled him to it. Eyes blinded by the wind-swept wisps of ghostly salt, he barely saw the speck appear on the horizon. Not a boat, nor a bird, but a house. Floating on the churning waves.

The boy woke.

In a bed. In a room.

Something tickled his cheeks, soft as eyelashes. It made him want to sneeze and left a damp, dirty smell in his nostrils. A high-pitched voice whispered urgently in his ears, 'Wake up, lad. Wake up!' and then was gone.

Beside his bed steamed a hot mug of tea. Tucked in his arms, a stuffed teddy bear was soft to the touch though it was worn and missing an arm. The boy had no idea where he was. No idea how he got there. No idea where he came from or what he was to do. Confusion was his only companion. All he remembered was a face, falling away from him into the whiteness. *Just a strange dream*, he thought.

The boy woke.

In the bed. In the room.

Outside, on the landing, he heard the creaking of a rocking chair. An old lady hummed as she tapped the knitting needles effortlessly back and forth, spooling coloured wool from the basket by her side.

'Hello, dear. Look what your Grandma has made you.'

As he pulled the woollen jumper over his head, the boy noticed the red weal of a scar healing on his wrist.

'Now off you trot and say hello to Grandpa Archie,' said Grandma.

The boy went to explore. The outer wall of the upstairs hallway was mostly gone. Beyond it was not tree or roof, but sea. An endless desert of salt water stretching as far as his eyes could see.

I must be hallucinating, he thought. *A house cannot float.*

Downstairs, he found a kitchen, with a large table and a wood-burning stove. On top of the stove was a kettle. Dotted around the floor were little traps.

'Ah,' said an old man, wiping his hands on a rag as he came in. 'That's for the flipping rat. He's a clever little tyke, but I'll get him yet.'

Next door to the kitchen was a workroom, full of

tools. He saw hammers and chisels, screwdrivers and planes. A hallway ran between the kitchen and the workroom with a cupboard and a staircase that led down into the cellar. But the cellar was underwater, lost to the gloomy sea that lapped at its steps.

The old man appeared at the foot of the staircase. 'Careful,' he said sternly. 'Best you stay upstairs, Jonah. Where it's safe.'

Oh, thought the boy. *My name is Jonah.* There was so much he couldn't remember. He knew what sea was, what sky was. He even knew why it rained and how to make fire out of dry twigs. All manner of interesting facts were right there at his tongue-tip. But when it came to where he came from or who he was, there was nothing.

The boy woke.

In his bed. In his room.

Downstairs, Grandpa Archie was at work in his den, sharpening a knife. 'There you go, lad,' he said, handing it over with a smile. The knife had a polished wooden handle carefully engraved with an embellished J.

'For Jonah,' said the old man, and handed him a piece of wood from the pile to play with.

The boy took the knife. 'Thank you,' he said.

'You always did love to carve,' said his grandma on the landing.

The boy woke.

A tap, tap, tapping sounded urgently from the floor below. He slipped out of bed and down the stairs, gripping his knife in his hand. The catch on the cupboard door had broken loose and the door was banging gently – tap, tap, tapping on the wall. The boy gave a start as he saw the huge figure lurking in its shadows. A great gleaming head and bowl-shaped eyes glistened in the light. Two huge hands hung by its side. It took a moment to realise that this was not a living thing. It was some sort of suit, built to hold a man and used to search underwater. *But to search for what?* he wondered.

As he fixed the latch with his knife, something caught his eye. In the dark pool of water that lapped the top of the cellar stairs, an eerie face drifted up from the deep, blonde and blue-eyed, and paler than the moon, the face stared back at him.

So, this is what I look like, he thought. *How weird to see your own face and not know it.* He reached a hand to touch the face in the water and a hand in the water reached to touch him. The dark mirror rippled and the face was gone.

Tired, the boy returned on tiptoes to his room. He crept back into bed and pulled a hair from his head. It was not blonde, but jet black.

The boy slept.

He dreamt of a looming metal man, huge gauntlet hands reaching for his throat. A blonde face peering from behind cold, dead eyes of glass, as rasping breath echoed in his ears. The gauntlet hands closed around his neck and he could hear something from behind the huge glass eyes. Something scratching. The scratching got louder, got closer. He could feel it now, running up his legs, his thighs, his chest ...

The boy jumped out of the bed, throwing the rat off him.

'Easy there!' said the rat. 'No need to freak out. Never seen a rat before?'

The boy must have. He knew what it was.

The rat began chattering. Words fell from its mouth so fast the boy had to work to keep up. He had not heard anyone speak more than a sentence or two since ... well, since ever he could remember.

'So, what'so the plan, kiddo? How we getting out of here? Build a boat? Rip a raft out of some of these roof beams? Let's get it together. Life is passing. Fun is being had and it's not us that's having it!'

'But I don't have a plan,' said the boy. 'I live here.'

The rat cocked its head. 'Yeah ... about that. You don't. Least you didn't. Trust me, I'd know. Name's Rodentia de la Rue, but you can call me Chippa. Been living here all my life. As in, here in the house, not here on the how-the-actual-tell-me-did-we-end-up floating on the ocean! And you, my friend, I can assure you, are a most recent arrival.'

'No,' said the boy, as panic rose in his chest. 'I've

always been here. With Grandma and Grandpa Archie.'

The rat shrugged. 'I don't know what to tell you, kiddo, but that ain't true. We been on the sail for long, long time before you showed your pretty little face – bang! Right out of nowhere. No boy one day, boy here the next. Shapah! Ooh, Magic!' She gave a little twirl and a look of wonder to the heavens, then shook her head. 'Not that I'm surprised. One night I go to bed as usual and next day, bam! I wake up and there's no land. No chimneys across the way. No squirrels throwing rotten nuts and insults from the tree next door. Just sea. And sky. And more sea. And sure, I've adjusted, but you know what? Fish and seaweed? Have you tried it? Goes right through ya! And there are days when it's so wet I stare up at the sun and just think, *Ooh! Snuggle me up, Sunshine. Swallow me up and fry me like a kipper!* That's how I'd like to go – and that ain't no lie. But I digress. Long and the short hair is … you don't belong here. I don't belong here. So, let's scram. Abandon the sinking ship-house and feel the sweet, sweet brush of the earth beneath our feet. What do you say, Matthew? You and me. Misfits for life.'

'My name isn't Matthew,' said the boy. 'It's Jonah.'

'You sure?'

He wasn't. A strange feeling rose in his chest.

The rat closed her eyes and touched his cheek. 'Let me see, I'm getting a … it's an M … and an A … with a T … definitely a … Ta da!'

With a flourish, Chippa pulled a slim white band of

bracelet from behind her ear. The boy looked to his wrist. The red weal was now so faint it was almost gone. But the white band fit the scar exactly. And on it, in dark pen and block letters, was the name MATTHEW M … The rest was all smudged.

'Old man cut it off and threw it away. Reckoned it might be important, so I rescued it. You're welcome.' She took a little bow.

'But how can you be sure that's my name?' he asked.

'Well, why else would you be wearing it? Unless … ooh! Is it someone else's?' She wiggled her tail and blew kisses to an imaginary friend then burst into laughter. 'Okay. Enough of the comedy,' she said, snapping out of it. 'Let's go, go, go! Build. Boat. Bye.'

'But I don't know how to build a raft,' said Matthew. 'And anyway, where would we go? I don't even know where we are. I don't even know if this really is my name.' He threw the bracelet on to the bed, more confused than ever.

Chippa placed her little paw upon his hand. 'Hey, it's okay. Stick with me, kiddo. Clueless or shoeless, we are getting off this floating House of Horrors, you mark my words.'

*

When Matthew awoke later that night, the rat had gone. In place of her scratching paws there was the rasping noise. Grabbing his knife once more, Matthew crept quickly past Grandma sleeping in her chair next to Archie's empty cot. Downstairs, the cupboard door was open. Inside was no underwater suit, just a large tank, the source of the rasping gasp. On the side of the tank was a dial, its little hand jabbing desperately into the red. A long pipe ran from the tank down the cellar steps into the blackness. Something pulled at the pipe urgently, trying to yank it free.

Something was terribly wrong. The suit and Grandpa Archie were both gone. Was it him pulling at the pipe? Was he in danger? Should he tell Grandma? Find Chippa? There was no time. No time meant no choice. With no thought for himself, Matthew stepped into the pool, taking the deepest breath he could, as the dark waters closed above his head.

He followed the pipe underwater into a child's playroom with a rusted bunkbed. Next to it was a rotted wooden fort. Opposite, by a broken window, was a large wardrobe which had fallen over. The pipe lay trapped underneath and Matthew could see Grandpa in the diving suit, his body wedged below the window. He could just make out the old man's face inside, blood smudged on his brow. He wasn't moving. The way the pipe was trapped, he could tell there couldn't be much air, if any, getting through.

As Matthew tapped on the glass of the helmet, something whipped through the broken window.

Something big. He wanted to look, but didn't have time. He knew he had to lift the wardrobe enough to free the pipe and let the old man breathe. He dove deeper to get a good grip on the underside. He pulled with all his might. Once. Twice. Soon, he knew, his body would panic and drag him back to the surface. He strained until he thought his shoulders would pop out of their sockets.

Not a move. Not an inch. Then ... Matthew felt the water swirl beside him and felt his burden lighten. The wardrobe rose and Matthew saw a large seal underneath, push the heavy oak box up on top of its broad shoulders. With the wardrobe lifted, Matthew pulled the tube out of the way. The wardrobe sank back to the floor. The seal darted over the top to grab the old man with its teeth. Pulling him as effortlessly as a rag doll, it swam toward the cellar steps.

Matthew's lungs screamed. He bolted out of the door and swam as fast as he could. His head throbbed and his vision blurred. He couldn't hold his breath a second longer. A rush of cold, salt water filled his lungs, flooded them full of the very thing they didn't want. His limbs thrashed – and were still. Panic subsided and a feeling of calm crept over him like a warm blanket. He was floating, suspended in the darkness. A shadow rippled at his side. Vaguely, somewhere at the back of his head, Matthew wondered what it was. The boy from the stair pool. Blonde-haired and blue-eyed and about the same age as him. His blue eyes were full of wonder and concern. In his hand he held a toy bear's stuffed arm.

Oh, I see, thought Matthew. *This is what the old man was searching for all along.*

And with that thought he drifted off to sleep. In the strange old house, under the long, plain stairs in the cold, dark water.

'At the edge of the sea by a lake of stars

A mirror and a tower shine from afar

Holding the key to a thousand doors

As two moons shine on ghostly shores.'

Who is that singing? wondered Matthew as the haunting melody woke him, tingling his flesh and soothing his bones.

'There he is!' Chippa the rat scurried up his chest and propped her front paws on his chin for a good sniff. Then she turned to address someone. 'All fine and dandy,' she announced.

Sitting next to them was a beautiful woman. Tight grey curls lay damp on her forehead. Her fur coat glistened, as if she had been dancing in the rain. Her huge, black eyes were fixed upon him and her pretty mouth smiled as she hummed.

'The sleeping prince awakes,' she said with a twinkle.

Matthew glimpsed her perfect white teeth, sharp as needles. He struggled to push himself up onto his arms.

'Don't worry,' said the woman, reading his mind. 'Your friend is fine. Listen.'

Grandpa Archie's throaty snore rumbled through the

house. 'Although I don't know how you could sleep with such a noise.'

'Tell me about it!' chipped in Chippa.

It was a very loud snore, Matthew had to admit.

By her side, the woman held the old man's diving helmet. She lifted it up. 'And who would have thought? It was just a man in a skin all along!' And with that she roared with laughter, although it was more like a peal of bells than a roar. A sound that lifted Matthew's spirits like a mouthful of sugar. 'And it never occurred to me. To me!' Her laugh gently slowed, like ripples fading on a summer lake. 'That was very brave of you; to try and rescue him.'

'Was it you who helped?'

'Yes. I'm Tersi. I've been watching out for you.'

Matthew sat bolt upright. 'There was a boy! Under the water. I saw him. We have to …'

'Shhhh.' She stroked his wet hair. 'He's fine. He was just a bit frightened. His name is Jonah.'

'That's the name of the little boy who lived here,' said Matthew. It was beginning to make sense now. 'I think he must have died.'

Tersi nodded and Matthew watched as droplets fell from her silver curls. 'He did. But he didn't want to leave his grandma and grandfather. He's been waiting for them to find him.'

'And Archie has been searching. And Grandma, she cries for him in her sleep.'

'He's been here all along. But he was scared of the big monster with the claws and the empty eyes. Every time he saw it, he would hide. But I think they will find each other now. And perhaps find some peace.'

'That's good,' said Matthew. He was pleased for them. But was anyone looking for him? he wondered. And if they were, how would he even know, when he remembered nothing before his time in the floating house?

'So, I really don't belong here,' he said.

'No. You don't belong here, it's true,' said Tersi, stroking the hair out of his face. 'But I think you knew that.'

Matthew nodded.

'Ah, so it goes, eh? I see.' Chippa sat back and put her hands on her hips. 'Don't believe it when I tell you, but now *she* says it?'

'I didn't want to be alone,' said Matthew.

The rat tickled his cheek with her whiskers. 'Hey, kid, you ain't ever alone. Not while I'm with ya! We're a team. Official. Rat and boy. Conquer the Birl!'

'You fell,' said Tersi. 'From the sky. Days ago. From where, I cannot tell. But I know someone who might. I think perhaps it's time to take you to see him, young Matthew. I've been looking out for Jonah. Keeping him safe. But now he won't need me any more.'

Matthew felt himself smile, for what felt like the first time ever. 'Thank you. I'd like that,' he said.

Chippa coughed loudly. '*Us*. Take *us* there. Team. Conquer. Birl. Remember? Sheesh.'

*

That night Matthew left the House that Sailed with Chippa in his pocket. Before he departed, he carved a heart on the floor and the words 'thank you' underneath for the old couple to find. By the cellar steps he placed the stuffed bear, his missing arm upon his lap, still wet. It pointed towards the rippling pool, where a young boy named Jonah waited to greet them.

Against the Tide
by Angela Jameson

In Chapter Ten of Against the Tide, Maggie's father meets Henry Templeman who has recently come to Whitby to find work. Henry has never sailed, but he is keen to get involved with the lifeboat. During a frank conversation about his responsibilities as coxswain of the lifeboat, John finds Henry a sympathetic listener and confides that his family have been raised in an unconventional way. Afterwards, when John discusses the encounter with his brother Will, both men are unsure whether Henry is friend or foe.

Across the water, on Pier Road, John crouched on the roof of the neglected boathouse. He perched with his heels under his haunches and bent his head over his work. One by one, he hammered the nails into place before making a minute adjustment to his position to address the next few out-of-place tiles. The coarse, thick skin of his hands was a hindrance when it came to doing close work like this; there was no sensitivity left in his fingers and he had already dropped more than a few nails before he'd managed to get a purchase on the wooden truss.

He should have enlisted his eldest to do this.

Ed had always been more inclined to the work of a craftsman than that of a fisherman, if truth be told, but until Thomas and Robert were much older, Ed's place was in the coble with John and Will. Today was Saturday though, and Maggie had coaxed Ed to go out in the boat with her while it wasn't being used for anything else. John smiled to himself. She had seen an opportunity and had persuaded him to let them use the boat – it was a half-holiday and, for once, the weather was in favour of sailing.

John had his own reasons for agreeing to this arrangement. It was a source of constant dismay to him that his own son did not possess the same aptitude for sailing as his daughter. Enough time in mourning had passed now since Beth had died and he needed Ed to take every opportunity to build up his rowing strength and, hopefully, working alongside his sister might sharpen up his sailing skills. John never ceased to wonder how, when he and Beth had brought them up as equals, taught and trained them in the same ways, Maggie had clearly inherited his own natural instinct for managing a boat, while Ed had not.

How was it that his daughter should be able to read the shifts in the winds and the tides as if it were her second nature, while his son, who needed these very skills for his own livelihood and to support his father, struggled to even tell bow from stern?

Such were the unanswered questions circling in John's mind when he heard someone calling his name from below.

He quickly took out the nails from between his lips

and called down. 'Hullo? Who wants me? I'm up here!'

After waiting for a response and hearing none, he resigned to descend from the roof to investigate who was calling him. By the time he had negotiated the ladder and had his feet firmly planted on the ground, John was not best pleased to find the door of the boathouse ajar. He always kept it shut if no one was working inside. He was suspicious of anyone that came here without a prior appointment, and when he squinted to adjust his eyes to the dim light, John was displeased to see a broad figure stooping to move a pail that had been strategically placed on the floor. Whether he knew this man or not, the intrusion was not welcome.

'It was there for a reason,' John said, with no hint of humour.

The figure calmly replaced the pail, drawing himself up to his full height as he turned to face John. The interior of the boathouse was dark, with only one door half open. The shaft of light that entered shimmered with particles of dirt and dust in the air and it was difficult to make out the features of the man before him, but John could estimate that he was at least a foot taller than himself and a good deal broader.

He took a step back and held on to the edge of the door. He couldn't be sure, but he thought this might be the fellow he'd been hearing rumours about. Pete Leadley had mentioned a giant of a man who'd started work in Barrick's shipyard a few weeks ago. Someone had joked about him having been a brick-worker previously: 'He looked like something built from bricks himself, he wa' that sturdy!'

The stranger thrust his hand in the direction of John's.

'Henry Templeman, at your service.'

Templeman – that was it. John recognised the name. He eyed the outstretched hand but didn't move an inch.

'I've no work, if that's what you've been sent for. This boathouse is property of Whitby Lifeboat Association. There's no jobs.'

Henry dropped his hand to his side. 'Sent for?'

The stranger's jovial smile remained. Was this man mocking him? He seemed to find the situation amusing.

'Well, if I was sent at all, it must have been the coastguard sent me; at least he was the one who told me where to find you. In truth, though, nobody "sent" me here and it's not work I'm about. I asked about town for you by name and I came here of my own free will. You are John Scott, I believe?'

'I am.' John opened the boathouse door a little wider and held his arm out to one side to indicate that Henry should come outside.

'Well then,' said Henry as he stepped out into the daylight, 'I hear you are the helmsman of the Whitby Lifeboat, and I'm keen to be of help here in any way I can.'

Now they were outside, John could see Henry's face

in the full light of day. He wore the complexion of a man who knew the outdoor life, that much was obvious, and his gaze was as clear and direct as his words. John allowed his guard to drop a little.

'You heard right. I am the coxswain of the lifeboat, and I have crew enough to fill two boats twice over even when there's no pay.'

'I think you misunderstand my reason for coming here today,' Henry went on. 'I have no wife and no children; I earn what I need up at the shipyard and I'm not looking for more pay. I want only to help with the lifeboat.'

John forced a laugh, but its bitter undertone was audible. 'Well, that's just as well! Often as not the lifeboat crew take no pay. The only money as comes our way is when Lloyds of London sees fit, and that's not often, since more than half the owners of the ships we salvage have never paid their dues. That's lifeboat life for you – plenty of graft, but no money.' John paused and then changed his line of enquiry. 'How are you with a boat? Do you sail?'

'I am no sailor. My father was a brick maker as was his father before him. But a man can learn, I think?'

John almost scoffed in response: 'You're wanting to learn what most men round here learned before they could walk! The lifeboat crew are all Whitby fishermen and they know this coastline and these seas as well as they know their own hands.'

For a few minutes, neither man spoke. John was considering how many folk were needed to move the boat on its carriage before a launch and the sheer manpower it took to lower it down the slipway to the sand. At least ten men were required to brace while another ten moved it forward; he could little afford to turn down this giant's offer of help, even if he wasn't a sailor.

'You've got the shoulders on ye. I can see you might be some use in a storm. But you'll need to learn how to handle a boat before I would ever let you in this one and you'll need to find a man with time to teach ye. Not many as I know'd be willing … You'd be taking their chance of a ticket, see?'

John paused when he saw a look of bafflement spread across Henry's face.

He continued. 'When there's a shout, as the coxswain, I have to decide which men get a ticket to row in the lifeboat. I have to make sure we have a strong enough crew for the waves and the weather. And I have to be fair, because a shout might mean extra money. So if you were to get fit enough to get in the lifeboat, you'd be taking another man's place. You understand me?'

'Aye. I see the problem, right enough,' Henry said.

The two men looked at one another for several minutes before Henry spoke again.

'It sounds to me as if it would take a good many months before I could acquire the skills you need to row in the lifeboat. You must believe me when I say I'm not looking for more pay and I certainly have no wish to interfere or threaten anyone's livelihoods. I have my own reasons for wanting to help.'

John could not quite make this man out. He was an odd one for sure. He glanced up at the roof of the lifeboat house where he'd been working only a few minutes ago. He considered all the other work that had to be done, not just on the boathouse, but on the boat itself. He'd be a fool to turn this man away, especially as he spoke so earnestly of not wanting any pay.

'I will need to talk to some of the other men about it, but I think we can come to some arrangement. If you can help me out with this roof, and fixing up the boats, I will see about finding someone who has time to show you your way around a boat. There's plenty to learn, even just getting her in and out of the sea.'

Henry grinned and held out his right hand. 'You have yourself an apprentice.'

This time, reluctantly, John shook it.

The two men turned to look out towards the horizon then and Henry nodded towards a small coble bobbing in the breaking waves. Two figures were visible; one hauled the sail in, the other had his back to Henry and John and was using the oars to drive the boat onto the sands.

'What about those lads?' Henry said. 'They look competent. Perhaps they'd have time to show me the ropes?'

A heavy scowl spread like a storm cloud across

John's brow. 'Those lads, as you choose to call them, are two of my own. And they're not lads, either.'

'Not lads?'

'One of 'em's my daughter.'

Just then, the two distant figures jumped into the shallows and it was obvious now that one of them was indeed wearing a skirt. Together, the two heaved the coble onto the sand, leaning forward at an angle to counter the weight of the boat.

'Well, I never!' Henry exclaimed. 'I thought lasses weren't allowed to work on fishing boats!'

'They're not. It brings bad luck. But …' John sighed and shook his head, as if trying to get rid of an unwanted fly, before taking a deep breath and starting again. 'It being Saturday, they're not working, as such. Any other day, you'd be right. Any fisherman round here would turn back if he even saw a woman on his way to work, never mind as let one on their boat. Maggie — well, some people say I'm soft on her — but Beth, my late wife, wasn't from round here and she had different ideas. She said if you live by the sea, you need to know what you're up against — and a lass needs to sail as well as any lad.'

John paused and turned to watch Ed and Maggie. 'Not everyone round here agreed with Beth's way of thinking. She was a Quaker when I met her, see? She gave it up to become my wife — she wasn't allowed in the Meeting House once she'd chosen to wed in the Church. But she had her principles, and she was the mother of my children, so that's where we're at.'

'It sounds to me as if your wife was a level-headed woman. I'm sorry I never had the pleasure of making her acquaintance ...'

John nodded and glanced away. He wasn't sure why he had explained so much to this stranger and he thought he detected genuine sorrow in Henry's countenance.

'I am sorry for your loss, John. It must be a difficult time. I don't have a family of my own, or even a wife, but I know what it is to lose someone you love. I can only imagine it is a dreadful hardship to bring up your family without a wife.'

John glanced back at Henry. His eyes shone with sincerity, but John flinched from holding his gaze. He had never been good with words and now they completely failed him. A few uncomfortable moments passed before John could even think how to move on. He had never met Henry Templeman before in his life, but within a few brief minutes of talking, the fellow had touched the raw agony in his chest. When John glanced up again, he was grateful to see that Henry had now shifted his gaze to the floor between them.

At last, John cleared his throat. 'Yes. Beth was level-headed, that's true.'

He stepped over towards the ladder leaning against the boathouse. He suddenly wanted to get on with things. But once he started moving, his words returned.

'Beth knew what was right and fair. Even when

others said something wasn't the done thing, she would do it anyway. She was always quite sure of herself. She wasn't like other women, airing their business along with their washing. If she had a problem, she kept quiet. She took herself off for a walk on her own. She had a sense of her purpose and she could make her mind up on her own. Without that … without her … yes, life is difficult.'

At this, the two men finally looked each other directly in the eye. Henry gave a sad, understanding nod.

'I'll put these tools away and come back later,' John said. Henry picked up the nails and hammer and followed him inside the boathouse.

As he locked up, John smiled.

'When we were courting, you know, I'd take Beth out in the boat sometimes. And Beth being Beth, she wanted to know everything. We used to laugh about how different our lives had been. I taught her about my way of life and she set me straight about a thing or two! Maybe if I hadn't listened to her, maybe if I hadn't let her have things her way, we wouldn't be where we are now …' He tailed off as he saw Will striding towards them.

'Are you alright, John? I was across the way and I saw you come down off the roof. Are you done for the day?'

He was speaking to John, but the whole time, he eyed the man at John's side with deep suspicion.

'I'm not quite done,' said John. 'I've a few more holes to deal with, but I'll see to them later. I'm going down to speak with Maggie and Ed.' Then he turned to Henry.

'Henry, this is my brother, Will. Will, this here is Henry Templeman. He's come to offer us some help around here.'

'That's right,' Henry stepped forward and extended his hand.

Will shot John a look before accepting a handshake. 'Will Scott. I think I've heard you mentioned – working up at Barrick's, are you?'

'I was just telling Henry,' John said, 'before anyone helps out with the lifeboat, I need to discuss it with you and the rest of the crew.'

'Aye. That's how it is.'

John pressed his lips together and nodded. He could sense from Will's abrupt manner that any discussion was closed for the time being.

Henry touched the brim of his hat and nodded at each of the brothers. 'Well, it was a pleasure to make your acquaintance. I know you must have a lot to do and discuss, so perhaps I'll meet Maggie and Ed next time?'

As soon as Henry was out of earshot, William clapped his hand on his brother's back. 'It looks like I arrived just in time, eh? I hope you told him we can't pay him. We don't even pay ourselves for half the work we do.'

'Don't worry. I set him straight on that score,' said John. Then he added, 'He seems a decent enough fellow, you know?'

'I do *not* know! How can you know when you've only

just met the chap? And what does he want with Maggie and Ed? What's Maggie doing down on the sands, anyway? Jane is on her own back in our yard and those little ones are running circles round her. There's plenty for a young woman to do at home, Saturday or not.'

John didn't like Will's tone; what Maggie should or should not be doing was none of Will's business. John still hadn't forgotten what Will had said the night of Beth's funeral. It rankled him, especially as some of what he'd said had since been proven right. John knew more changes were needed, but he wasn't prepared to admit it just now.

'Maggie's with Ed. I asked her to help him with a few tasks.'

This was half true. The more Ed spent time in the boat with Maggie, the more dependable he would be when the three of them were working.

'I see,' said Will. 'I didn't think I saw her with the other lasses, that's all. Polly and Nancy and a couple of others are mooning about up on the bridge. You know what they're like when they've got their eye on somebody? Like seagulls following a catch. I wouldn't be surprised if it's Henry Templeman they were waiting for. We shall have to keep an eye on him.'

'Why? Do you know something about him that I should know?'

John was starting to feel anxious he had told Henry too much.

'Nothing out of the ordinary. Only that he's taken lodgings in town and is working up at one of the shipyards.'

'Nothing untoward? No reason to believe he's dishonest?' John tapped his jacket pocket for the jingle of his keys.

'As I say, nothing out of the ordinary. But unless the man gives me reason to trust him, he's only as bad as the next one that comes off the boat. One of the lads heard he's been working for a farmer up at Danby for years and was courting the farmer's daughter. Then the family suddenly up and took a boat to Canada. Left him high and dry. Make of that what you will, but I would think twice before I let him make my daughter's acquaintance.'

John's forehead furrowed. He chided himself for not being more thorough in his questions to Henry. 'That could be something or nothing, Will. Plenty of people get on the boat in the hope of finding a better life elsewhere – many of 'em Yorkshire farmers as well. It's probably nothing to do with Templeman. Or the farmer's daughter. Perhaps he is saving for a ticket so he can follow his sweetheart? He seemed honest enough and since he's staying in Whitby and he's willing, I don't see why we shouldn't make use of him.'

'Hmmm. Well, the rest of the men will have something to say about it.'

'I'm sure they will, but unless they want to fix this boathouse up, I'm not inclined to listen.'

Geissberg
by Daphne Mays

Part One
Chapter One

'I am lost! All of my things are lost!' a disembodied, struggling voice shouts in the distance. His cry starts softly but increases in sound until the word lost, is piercing: 'I am verloren! All of my things are verloren.'

I look with alertness toward the sound of the voice but am unable to see a soul. Eager to get my family's reactions, I turn towards my husband Heiri who's sitting on a tree stump by the campfire, listening to my daughter Gritli and son Ueli telling each other silly jokes. They are all holding sticks that they found in the woods on our way up the Geissberg mountain. The sticks have Cervelat sausages stuck to the ends which they're cooking over the open fire.

'Can you hear that?' I ask my husband. 'It sounds like that man is in trouble.' The corners of Heiri's lips begin to curl involuntarily when he hears one of the jokes his kids have told, and it looks like he is trying hard to hold back the laugh as his cheeks swell momentarily under pressure. Still, his laughter erupts, echoing through the woods as he bends over, slapping his knee repeatedly.

'Hey, I'm talking to you!' I say, my eyebrows scrunching together.

I try to catch my husband's attention by pushing him, but I stumble. My hands fall right through him onto the floor.

Lying on the ground, my eyes dart around towards the campfire. But there is no one sitting by the camp any more. The fire is out.

What is going on here? Was I imagining my family? Am I dreaming?

But it doesn't feel like a dream.

I hurry along through the woods, looking between the trees and down the gravel paths with gnarled roots dipping into and out of the ground, trying to find this poor man. Maybe he has lost his map on his hike and needs help finding his way back. But I can't find the guy. My family is also nowhere in sight. All I can see are the trees.

Standing by the Geissberg mountain viewpoint, I clutch onto the metal railings as I look down over the rock face at the village of Rüfenach. The houses have gabled roofs with large windows flanked with shutters and flower boxes. Visible from far away, the Romanesque church with a blue steeple, sits on a rock by the river Aare.

Where are you all? You've got to be here somewhere. I can see a ghost-grey mist swaddling the village below. It rises like the steam from running water in a bathtub until I can only see the snow-covered mountains and the church tower in the distance.

It is eerily silent, apart from the man's cries in the woods.

The trees are swaying, the leaves rustling in the breeze. They are all different shades of green: some are still budding, a fresh, lime-green colour, whilst the full leaves are a lush emerald under the overhead sun. Rays of warm sunlight filter through the uninterrupted layer of foliage, creating a pattern of light on the ground.

I rub the back of my neck, not knowing where to search next. What if the man has fallen over and injured himself? He might need medical help. I cannot ignore his cries for help and leave him alone on the mountain. Looking back down towards the village, the ghostly scarves of mist have wrapped themselves around the woods. It looks like a maze. Nothing escapes the mist: it traps every field and tree without mercy.

I enter the maze. I need to help the vulnerable guy, get him back home, and find my family. The trees overshadow me; their branches are twisted and lumpy, like grabbing fingers. I look up over the thick, dark trunks rising steadily into the sky, their branches joining with their neighbours' like giant arms connecting to protect their homes. The trees are densely packed together, leaving just enough space to allow someone to manoeuvre through. I am sweating like mad, even though

45

the air is cold. Because the mist has covered all the trees, no cracks are left for the sun to shine through and illuminate the path. The underbrush is so dense I can barely walk through the woods without getting my clothes torn on the branches. A thick carpet of leaves is muffling my footsteps. With my hands stretched out in front, I am struggling to make my way as the overhanging tree limbs smack me in the face. Wind whistling through the branches makes the leaves howl in a bone-chilling symphony.

There is a campsite up ahead, which I have visited many times. I may find the man there. There is always the possibility of this situation being something stupid, like him having lost his sausages and now expressing anger at himself for his carelessness. With my hand in front of my face, pushing the last branches aside and making my way through to the campsite, I end up standing before an unknown gravel path, exactly where it used to be.

Did I take a wrong turn somewhere? As a child, I often walked up the Geissberg mountain and thought I knew the mountain's paths off by heart. It made me the best candidate to find the man. But this is the first time I have seen this gravel path.

I am ill at ease, restless like a leg that can't stop bouncing under the table, imagining that something terrible might happen.

The air is thick with the scent of damp earth, and I can't shake the feeling that I am being watched; perhaps by the man I am looking for.

My skin tingles. I feel like I have been searching in the woods all day and have lost track of time because I am not wearing a watch, and the church is nowhere in sight. I must wait for the church bells to ring to know the time. In the canopy, birds are twittering, chirping, and calling in distant melodies to their kin, flying from tree to tree. I can hear a faint rustling as squirrels scamper through the foliage and hurry over thousands of breakable branches, though it is drowned out by the greater rustling of the leaves in the gentle breeze. Every rustle and every creaking branch makes my heart race with fear.

'I am lost! All of my things are lost!' I can hear the panicked man again.

I start to scream back. 'I'm coming. Hang on.'

I hope he can hear me, and it will calm him down somewhat. His cries are getting louder, and I am optimistic I am heading in the right direction. But the deeper I go, the more the mist seems to close around me. The trees are growing thicker, and the underbrush is tangled. The sounds of the outside world are fading away, leaving me alone with the mystery of the man and the absence of my family.

The mist is dancing around me. Am I daydreaming? I quicken my pace, desperate to find him. Pushing deeper into the heart of the woods, I know I am taking a risk. But the allure of helping a vulnerable man is too strong to resist. And so, I move forward, my heart beating faster with each step. I have no idea what lies ahead, but I have to find out.

Suddenly, I trip on a bumpy root and land flat on my face. Turning over onto my back, I look at the mist with wide eyes. But there is no pain in my body. Trying to stand up, not knowing how badly the fall has injured me, I feel water droplets run down my upper lip. Believing the droplets have fallen from the leaves above, I try to wipe them off with my t-shirt. At that moment, I see a blood smear on the fabric. A shudder of disbelief runs over me as the reality of the situation sinks in. Touching my upper lip several times with my fingertips, I hope it is my imagination, but red liquid trickles down my fingers. Oh my God, what am I going to do? A sudden pain surges through my legs, and when I look down at them, I see purple with blue blotches covering my knees. Trying to hold onto a tree and stand up, the pain is too intense. I sit with my back against a tree, sighing, and trying to clean my upper lip wound with leaves. I don't know what to do. I am all alone. Tears are welling up in my eyes and rolling down my cheeks.

'I am verloren! All of my things are verloren!' That voice again.

'Oh, shut up. You are the fucking idiot that got me into this situation.' I cry.

Instantaneously, I hear leaves crackle and branches snap next to me. Hearing the faint sound of something moving in the distance, my imagination runs wild with visions of beasts and monsters hiding in the shadows. Trying to block my imagination, I rapidly turn my head. Right now, it is just me at the mercy of Mother Nature. There is nothing else to be concerned about. But what is that? I see a shadow emerging from the woods. It starts slowly heading towards me.

'Is that you, lost man? It's funny how we both managed to get ourselves in a similar situation. But I'm glad we can now meet and help each other get back home. Sorry for cursing you before. As you can see, I'm not in the best state.' As the shadow appears out of the mist, it has a black and white face like a chess board and piercing black eyes. Seeing its vertical sharp horns, I scream in anguish.

Chapter Two

I burst out laughing when I see a four-legged creature running away from me, disappearing back into the mist, probably shocked by the scream I just let out. I completely forgot that the mountain is called Goat Mountain for a reason, and a chamois just came to say hello to me. I hear a sound like a bird flapping its wings in a panic. Maybe it's the sound of my heart. It reminds me of a wild bird looking for a way out of a cage. I am sitting on the floor, lightheaded, and my skin is cold and sweaty. I am sobbing uncontrollably and hugging my knees, rocking back and forth. I cry out, 'God, why? Why don't you love me?'

Still in shock, I descend the mountain by sliding my bottom on the leaves because my legs still hurt too much to stand up. Even though the mist is present, the light still shining through the trees turns a gravel-grey colour. This colour blots out any view of the woods as I try to slide down to the village. The darkness grows ominous. I hope the trees will shelter me and I can see out the shower. But then droplets begin to drip from the leaves.

Now, the rainfall is more intense and sounds like a crackling fire. Like things can't get any bloody worse! Why is life punishing me for trying to help a poor guy? I let out a loud shriek and start hitting my fists onto the leaves on the ground. Only one thing is on my mind: how to get home. I'm not scared; I can fight back if something happens. I imagine an angel, coming down from heaven to pick me up. I can see it taking me home and having dinner with my family. But at the same time, I feel hopeless.

I shout their names, hoping they can hear me: 'Heiri! Gritli! Ueli!' Oh, please get me out of this horrible mess! Tears are spilling over and flowing down my face, merging with the rainwater. 'Heiri! Gritli! Ueli!'

The darkness feels heavy and oppressive. I soon find myself swallowed up in nothingness, unable to see my two hands in front of my face. I can't make out where the sky and the ground are any more. What is up and what is down? I can feel wet leaves on the floor, but how can I be sure I am not by a cliff or hanging from a tree? I have utterly lost any sense of direction. The colour before my eyes isn't complete darkness but a colour that reminds me of space. I can still see my life stretching endlessly before me, but there is nothing I can do to improve the situation; I can take no action but wait for a moment I may never know. Am I as lost as the lost guy? Is this the torture he is enduring? Am I now in his shoes?

The rain is freezing and paling my skin on contact. With my clothes gradually increasing in weight, it encumbers my progress. But I continue to scramble for hope. I persevere in anticipation of soon arriving back at the village. Feeling my way through the branches and bushes, I feel this sudden stinging pain in my hands all down my arms. It feels like bees stinging me all over my body. *Oh, for fuck's sake.* But I can't have got myself caught in a beehive. They live up in the trees – unless the beehive has fallen from the tree. Or I am up on the tree. But I don't hear any humming. Nor do I feel any ants crawling across my body.

The pain is so severe.

I run my fingers over my skin and can feel lumps appearing. The stabbing pain won't disappear, and my body starts to itch. I try to stay sitting upright and summon strength, and for a brief moment, I do. Then my posture betrays me, and my only sense is of the cold, wet leaves against my damp hair.

Ding, ding. Ding, ding.

I can hear tinkling in the distance. What's that? It sounds like a call bell at a hotel reception. The continuous ringing gives me hope again that a hotel might be nearby. *Ding, ding. Ding, ding.*

The sound is getting louder and I start to realise I am hearing the church bells ringing. They are striking the hour. Counting the number of strikes, they end at twelve. My mouth opens wide, and my body freezes. The woods were bright before as if it were daytime. Is it nighttime now? How long have I been in the woods? Oh my God! I must have passed out at some point. Rummaging through my thoughts, trying to make sense of everything, thinking I have closed my eyes, I can see a cold white light shining through the trees. It blinds me like headlights on a dark road. I have been overwhelmed by darkness before, but now I am blinded by an empty eternity gleaming over me.

'Mrs Beldi?' a concerned male voice shouts from the direction of the light.

I swiftly sit up, banging my head on a branch.

With my hand on my forehead in pain, I answer, 'Yes.'

I see two police officers wearing black uniforms: a man and a woman.

'We've been looking all over for you for ages! What have you been doing?'

Relieved to see them and now thankfully in safe hands, I reply, 'I went to look for a guy who shouted he was lost in the woods. He sounded like he might need medical help. Did you find him? If not, he may still be in the woods. My family is also nowhere to be found.'

'Let's get you sorted out first.'

Did someone report me missing?

The police officers help me onto my feet and we walk down the mountain, with me holding onto them like crutches.

In the distance, I can now see lights in the windows of a five-storey building. The Swiss flag sways in the wind on top of the roof. A monumental staircase stands at the entrance. Once we arrive at this beautiful place, I read on a plaque the name of the hotel: *Geissberg – Welcome to Happiness*. I have lived here all my life, and in the twenty-eight years I have been here, I have never noticed such a majestic hotel looking over Rüfenach.

Unholy Sea
by Jacqueline Smith

Part One

God dwells in the hearts of all beings, Arjuna: thy god dwells in
thy heart. And his power of wonder moves all things – puppets in
a play of shadows – whirling them onwards on the stream of time.
– The Bhagavad Gita

Sanur, Bali
January 1992

On the third day after Nyepi, the frangipani tree lost all
of its flowers and Pak Yasser considered the possibility
that the good spirits had abandoned him and his home.

He crouched before the fire, watching the smoke
dance through the air, sweeping first past the kitchen
utensils hanging from a piece of bamboo, then by the
huge cooking pot perched on its throne of stones. He
liked to sit and think at this early hour when the only
interruption was the sound of cocks crowing. The village
still sleepy, fires lit and verandas swept, the air still and
cool. He looked around his home. The frangipani tree by
the main entrance had been bursting with blossoms a few

days earlier, but now the ground beneath was littered with discarded flowers, a scented carpet, wafting the sweet, sickly smell out towards him. High on the wall surrounding the compound, Vishnu, god of water, stared down at him. Maybe it was the distance and Yasser's poor eyesight, but the god's stony expression looked different this morning. He shifted position, his stomach clenching.

The veranda leading to his bedroom was in front of him, the dirt path trailing through the garden to the lowered bamboo screens. Behind them, his wife Sri would soon be waking. He worked the bitter betel nut paste between his teeth before spitting it out, its dark red stain melting into the ground. Early Morning Light joined him where he squatted and hummingbirds hovered, shimmering blurs of blue and green.

He picked up the book: it was thin, green and leatherbound. As he opened it, two pages fell to the ground, one a drawing, the other a photograph. The wax drawing was of the sea, indigo and emerald.

The photograph was of a young woman, and as he peered at it, he saw it was Lara. Wearing diving gear, she was perched on the edge of a boat, ready to drop into the sea behind her. She was smiling but looked tiny, swamped by the equipment and tanks surrounding her, tubes of rubber snaking out from under her legs.

Squinting, Pak Yasser tried to make out the words in front of him. They were faded and the pages wrinkled and dusty, but he could see it was a diary or journal from the dates at the top of some of the pages. He knew that he needed glasses but, he thought to himself wearily, needing something and being able to afford something do not always occur at the same time. He sighed, rose and walked over to the 'tourists' house', with its proper front door and concrete walls, rather than bamboo screens. He'd found the book on the bedroom floor and now struggled down to see if there was anything else underneath the bed. Nothing – just a large spider curled up in the corner.

Cradling the journal to his chest, he decided to show it to his daughter, Madé. She'd read it to him and, more importantly, she'd know what to do with it. Thick rays of sunlight cut across his path as he stood on the step of the guest room, and he heard the sound of a gecko scuttling up the wall behind him.

In the distance the sea trembled, light shimmering on its surface. Divers. Were they brave or foolish, he pondered. It had always seemed an odd occupation to him. But then he was Balinese and so had always known that the sea is unholy. The place where monsters and demons dwell.

Singapore
New Year's Eve
1990

Peeling, pastel buildings with shutters open to the stifling heat and the scent of spice. The man's stomach rumbled as he looked down on people eating in the roadside restaurants, the bus almost grazing the pavement as it rushed through the narrow streets of Little India. There was an excitement and bustle in the air – it was New Year's Eve, after all. People everywhere, all going somewhere, movement and smiles. Colour and light. It still felt good to be away from the grey of London, even after travelling for weeks. No walls coming in on him, suffocating and narrow. He could breathe here. He didn't owe anyone anything, and he was free.

'Everything's getting grey, and it'll be greyer. But some places withstand the malady longer than you think.' Where had he read that? It didn't matter, the point was he was done with grey. The bus halted and he bent down, rummaging in his rucksack for his battered *Lonely Planet*. As he lifted it, a photograph fell onto his lap.

He was laughing in the print, his arm draped over the shoulder of a woman who was also beaming at the camera. Angela. Her black hair was cut into a short bob, her huge eyes framed in dark make up. Wiping the sweat away from his neck, he stopped short as a sharp twinge stabbed at the front of his head, prompting him to touch the scar hidden under his mess of hair. No, it was better this way. He couldn't do it, he wasn't ready to live in an office and sit in a tube to go to work every day, going home every evening to play at being married. It wasn't him, she should have known that, should have understood him, where he was from. Not pleaded and begged him to stay. He'd never promised her anything, had he?

He reached for his passport from the front of his backpack and turned to the photo page. Sam Trelawny, place of birth: Falmouth. Clamping the little leather book shut, he stuffed it back into his bag. It didn't even look like him any more. He could just about make out his image in the dirty window. Two months in Kathmandu meant that his hair hung long around his neck and stubble was threatening to grow into a beard. He'd better get cleaned up before tonight. Trust Rupert to book a table at Raffles.

*

'Where the hell is she?' Rupert turned to Sam, leaning forward to flick his ash into the tray.

'How would I know? She's your friend …'

'It's New Year's Eve, for God's sake. The least she could do is turn up …' Marie picked up her drink, turning the glass in her hand. 'Isn't my Singapore Sling pretty? It matches my dress.'

'It does indeed, my love, and may I say, Marie, you look stunning tonight. Sam, doesn't Marie look stunning?' Rupert was in full swing this evening. Sam smiled to himself. Dressed in his best suit, finished off with a paisley neckerchief and waving a long cigarette holder around, he looked as though he'd stepped out of the 1920s. Sam glanced down at his own suit, thankful that he'd found a tailor in Little India. Not as finished as Rupert's but it would do, and it fitted him. It felt odd to be in a suit after the last month of wearing old fisherman's trousers and scruffy t-shirts, but tonight called for it. He studied himself in the huge mirror that ran behind the whole length of the bar, turning his head to the side. The barber had done a good job.

'Sam ...' Rupert was waiting for an answer and so was Marie.

'Sorry, yes ... you look lovely, Marie,' Sam agreed. Marie actually *looked* like her Singapore Sling, her tight red dress clinging to her hips like the curves of a glass. She was wearing a miniature emerald fan in her hair, perched against her sleek black head, like the green umbrella propped against the side of her drink. Leaning towards Sam, she put on her best Singlish. 'What's wrong with you, lah?' Why you not dance wi' me?'

Rupert's chair scraped along the floor as he jumped up and headed off towards the huge wooden doors by the entrance of the bar. Sam saw a throng of men in naval uniform coming through and his flamboyant friend embracing someone amongst them. He stood up to get a better view. A girl, almost as tall as the men around her, was hugging him and laughing. Surrounded by a sea of dark-haired sailors, her white-blonde hair was extraordinary. They started to move towards the table.

She held out her hand to him, 'I'm Lara, and you're Sam, aren't you? Rupert told us you were coming to

59

Singapore.'

His face was suddenly warm.

'You can stop staring now, Sam,' Rupert said.

Marie and Rupert startled to giggle. Sam reached for his wallet from his jacket, slung over the bar stool. 'What can I get everyone to drink? My round.' It was as though the floor had shifted beneath him, and now he had to concentrate on every move.

'I think you'll find it's Slings all round!' Rupert yelled out as he dragged Marie onto the dance floor.

Sam headed to the bar, Lara next to him.

'Where were you earlier?' he shouted over his shoulder as they wove through the crowd.

'Teaching Japanese businessmen!'

'On New Year's Eve?'

'Yes, I know, but I didn't realise the dates when I signed up and I need the extra money.'

There was a crush at the bar and Lara's bare arm was cool against his skin, her long hair hiding her expression. He tried to think of something to say, his mouth dry. The spot where their skin was touching tingled.

'Listen, I can't hear anything in here,' he managed. 'Can we go out onto the veranda?'

The deck had one free table. He pulled a chair out for her, using his free hand to pull his shirt away from where it was sticking to his back.

'So, how long are you in Singapore, Sam?'

'Actually, I leave the day after tomorrow.' He leaned

towards her. 'I promised Rupert I'd come and see him. How has the old devil been?'

'He keeps us all laughing at school … he's a dear friend.'

She reached forward to pick up her drink, a silver charm bracelet sliding on her arm. Sam stared at it, the bracelet glinting on her pale skin and moved his hand towards her wrist. He touched her, turning her hand over in his. She didn't pull away. Her skin was cool, even in the heat.

'This is pretty … did you get it out here?'

'No, my grandmother gave it to me years ago. She lived with us when I was growing up. We were close.'

Her hands slapped the air just in front of his nose, forcing him to jerk backwards.

'Mosquito, sorry!' she laughed. He grinned, pushing the hair back off his forehead. The barber had left more on top than he wanted but it was a relief to feel what little breeze there was on his neck. He sat back in his chair, happy to let her talk. There was something calming about her face and the way she spoke – it was like listening to soothing music after the noise and chaos of the past few weeks. Then she stopped, and started to fiddle with her hair, wrapping it around into a bun at the base of her neck. Her cheeks were flushed.

Sam leaned forward. 'Can you scuba dive?' he looked into her eyes. The colour reminded him of the palest green sea glass, like the pieces he'd spent hours scouring the beach for as a child.

She smiled slowly. 'Yes, I haven't done a lot recently, but I learned when I was eighteen. My college had a club.'

'I'm going to Thailand to become a dive instructor.'

'That's cool, very cool ... lucky you ...' She leaned in, and her breath touched his face.

'There you two are!' Rupert appeared in front of them, looking less polished than earlier, his neckerchief unravelled and lipstick marks on his cheek. Sam had a sudden urge to punch him in the face, but forced a smile.

'Join us for the fireworks,' he beckoned. Behind him, Marie was waving and people were making their way out into the hotel garden.

Sam stood and reached for Lara's hand. She knocked back her drink, then took it. They joined the crowd just in time to see the sky explode in colour. Cheers and shouts filled the space around them, and everybody was hugging and kissing. He stood rooted to the ground, aware of the commotion around him, wanting to look at her but hesitating, trying to control his racing thoughts. Her hand on his arm.

'Aren't you going to kiss me? It's New Year's Eve!' Lara's mouth was by his ear, the whisper just loud enough. He looked at her, first at her eyes, then to her smiling lips, then back again. Her eyes were level with his even though she'd slipped off her heels. How strange to be with a woman almost as tall as him.

He pulled her out of the crowd and led her to a quiet

spot on the other side of the veranda. Taking her face in his hands, he kissed her gently on the lips. They stared at each other for a moment, his mind racing. What was happening to him? This was insane. Why now? It was too soon, wasn't it? Could he change his plane ticket? He wanted her, yes, but there was something else.

His mother's words popped into his thoughts. *Just remember, my darling, life can turn on a moment in time. Don't miss those moments.*

'Come with me.' A second passed. His words hung in the air. Had he really said that?

'What?' Lara shouted, her face lit up by another exploding firework, surprise in her eyes.

Sam's heart hammered in his chest. 'Come with me … to Indonesia.'

Lara opened her mouth and he waited for the words.

People moved around them, the music started up again in the hall. *Say yes.*

He looked from her eyes, he couldn't read them, to her mouth and back again. Slowly, she started to smile.

'Why not?'

Drifting
Jakarta
April 1991

Lara watched as he slept. From where she sat in the window recess, she could see a hole the size of a ten pence piece in the filthy mosquito net surrounding him. Like those curtains that hang in old houses. Probably hadn't been washed in years, she thought, returning to her journal. Turning the green book in her hands, she realised that, apart from her silver bracelet, this diary was probably her most precious belonging. As soon as she'd moved to Singapore, she'd bought it from a stationer's and started recording her new life. No mention of England or anyone there would be found on its pages – now Granny had gone, there was no need to remember.

Pulling her knees up to her chest, she stared out of the window. The street was busy below, traders setting up the daily market, the figures and stalls moving into position like performers in a carefully choreographed dance.

Her gaze returned to Sam. He was curled into a foetal position beneath the thin sheet, looking much younger than his twenty-four years. His hair, starting to bleach in places, was strewn across the pillow. It needed cutting but still he looked good, very good. She wondered how many girlfriends he'd had. She'd tried asking him one night but he'd brushed her off, changing the subject and then silencing her with a kiss. The truth was, she didn't really care. Something about him caught her right in the chest, made her giddy. She still couldn't believe that she'd given up her job to go travelling with him.

'Are you sure about this, Lara?' Her mother's anxiety barely hidden on the crackly line during their fortnightly telephone call.

'Yes, I'm sure.'

She'd felt like saying, 'Why do you care anyway? Now you're free to shack up with any useless shit that turns up, without me interfering.' She bit her lip instead. What was the point of upsetting her mum when she was so far away? The moment she'd clicked her seat belt on that flight to Singapore, she'd promised herself she would put the past behind her. As the wheels lifted off the tarmac, life in England became meaningless and she'd comfortably fallen into the cliché of travelling to forget. So far it had worked.

The floor next to the bed was strewn with maps, the largest annotated with big arrows and lines plotting out their journey. Sam already had it all planned out; their stopping points on the route from Jakarta to Bali circled in red. His battered copy of *Lonely Planet* sat bang on top of Java. She hardly knew this man and yet she trusted him, was willing to travel through unknown lands together. His 'let's go' attitude was addictive, and she was drunk on it. So what if she knew nothing about his past? She hadn't told him anything much about herself and didn't really want to. Why dredge up all of that when it was so good between them?

On that dreamlike New Year's Eve, she'd been swept away on the romantic idea of it all, but a few days later she hadn't really believed he'd come back. He'd taken her by surprise. Men, in her experience, didn't behave like this. After her father had left them, she'd watched as men had drifted in and out of her mother's life. Unreliable and uncommitted, all of them. Dangerous, too.

He was different.

Eve
by Linda Kay Stevens

'We are composed of agonies, not polarities.'
– James Hillman

Arrival

We arrived quickly in this dumpy little spaceship with its worn-down industrial grey carpet and outdated Star Trek engine room. Sure, it can cross time and space, but I can see boot-prints in space dust from previous guests.

This is the last stop before going home. Another stint-rota of repair and restocking, endless lists to be reviewed.

I always feel short of breath until I adjust the oxygen settings to humanoid levels, and it will take a couple of sun cycles to even-keel-spread throughout the ship. I must look at my watch to know the time of day as the sunrise-sunset program has yet to be switched on.

Dingy, dark, and cramped, my space-mate putters around, putting his temporary nest in order; a few graphic novels, a photo of his dog on Earth – why we can't bring Tuffy is beyond me – and the coffee mug that has our wedding picture on it.

I hit the loop-way and go for a jog. One benefit of low-gravity outer space is that it allows me to run on my two bad knees. As I start my laps, I notice the ceiling is beginning to slant in towards the floor. Quickly, it becomes so low that I can't get through without crawling on all fours. This disturbs me immensely – my claustrophobia, which has been held at bay, breaks through – and so I turn back only to notice water gushing through an exposed pipe that has burst where the curved wall meets the domed ceiling.

Alarmed, I turn back and yell for Adam, 'Come, grab your repair tools, hurry!'

I inflate our protective climate-shift garb and wait for him to save us.

Even now, in this potential danger zone, he putters. He doesn't trust my alarm bells; I can't blame him. I'm a high-strung Earth mama far from home, fresh from the nap tube, jumping to worst-case scenarios.

As we approach the anomaly, an unknown corridor strewn with neon orange chairs catches our attention. It's as if some raging teens have let loose at a high school bust-up. We follow the overturned furniture into a larger room filled with artificial light emanating from a humming neon tube below our feet. There, we see a few ageing humans silently shuffling about in beige-coloured papier-mâché jumpsuits; seniors in an Alzheimer's care home. They carry trays of colourless food heated in a microwave, and the smell fills my nostrils with bad memories.

We continue upwards until we see a stone spiral staircase leading to an enormous window; we head up to see the view. Someone has turned daylight on, and my breathing becomes less tight. It's amazing what a little psych-technology does for the lungs. Still, it's not real; flat and bird-less, one of the park trees is on the blink, its leaves going back and forth from Girl Scout green to autumnal crimson like an old Eat At Joe's diner sign.

I look down and notice a mound of cement, like wet sand, and bend down to touch it. It is as if, by memory, my hands begin to mould it into a palm-sized egg. Adam looks at me and tells me not to touch it; it could be dangerous. But something in me slithers; a wave in my belly, a feeling of ... happiness?

A few handmade and mottled orbs later, a growing pile of eggs surrounds me. They are the colour of beeswax, and the smell of frankincense fills the ship, which is now breaking apart. The egg mound continues to expand, becoming a hill with trees and animal creatures that crawl or fly, and I want to name them.

Bird, horse, turtle, dove, cat, cow, snake ...

My belly rumbles, then quakes, and I am filled with a pain that rises up and becomes a great yowling. I look down and see a giant mountain bursting forth from between my legs, and Adam is on his knees saying; *push, push, hold. Push, push, hold.*

Pandemic

Upstairs in my bed, now our bed, he lies dreaming. Coal-hot, fever-visions.

Climbing the stairs, I hoist my bad knee and lonely pussy, carrying electrolyte water and ice-cloths. His olive skin, now grey, coiled silver locks – once gleaming with almond oil and frankincense – now a snarl of empty nests.

I lay next to him and listen. His breathing is like shredded wind in a tunnel underground – medieval, plagued.

This is the turning of the plot, where the husband lies dying.

After days of febrile in and out of consciousness, he comes to, just for a moment, with a message. But before he can speak it, the wife-mouth trembles and spills out joy-words of I-missed-you-so-much and where-did-you-go and don't-leave-me-here-all-alone ...

There is only one breath moment for him to mouth, *I love you*. And whoosh, he is gone.

Runaway Meet-up

And the mother says, *Utah, where you were born.*

And the daughter-now-mother says goodbye to Texas, adios, Mama Frida, and Papa Abraham.

The exact midpoint between she and me, the now-daughter Eve, is a diner.

An in-between-Queendom that pours free coffee refills all day long.

The daughter stirs Mini Moo's into her java once-ebony-now-toffee-tone. Her hands, limp-wristed, give the menu back, while Mother orders liver and onions, medium-rare with scrambled eggs, moist. It was often the same weary-boned waitress, her eyes reflecting time lost, vacant as a parking lot on Christmas. Mother warns that if the eggs are overcooked, they'll be returned immediately.

More coffee arrives, and a where-did-we-leave off look from the daughter and the mother resumes her story.

The mother wonders if the daughter will eat, as she stirs a teaspoon of powered saccharine into liquid blackness.

An upside-down tornado is forming.

Utah the now-daughter says, remembering her false Eden, California, where her Lady Godiva mane was shorn and dyed the colour of Never-Found-Love.

Yes, Utah, the mother repeats, *where you were born.*

Reborn

I love you, Daddy mouthed through the only tears the mommy ever saw him cry. The Daddy was so happy when the Grandparents forgave them both – a Jewish girl and an Episcopalian boy – because the baby daughter looked like Abraham, hair red as a burning bush.

Potent Angel

A dark bride, a desert bride, a firstborn and cast aside bride.

Feet and hands painted gold with clay smelling of fresh rain and mushroom blooms.

A silk-talking woman, a velvet-wood woman whose winter light splits her open, filling her with ice salmon, lemons, and mint.

She hears the sun rising over the sea and feels the glint of peach and pearl in a blue god's eye.

They are guiding her as she sonic wing-seeks a forest to rest in, a single tree to nest in, but none are near.

A barn will have to do, slanted rafters overlooking pig babies, born and torn from ...

Nativity

Adam kneels, repeating *thank you, thank you* to my belly, and he catches our daughter. A baby girl lights the sky with a dream and the eruption of our gene pool. Volcanic blooms unfurl from her scalp, and she silently mouths *I love you* as my body bleeds into the sea, forming land now a beach, and our sunburnt shoulders fold over and look for shells.

Charwoman, whose lightning strikes the high watch and turns the boat around.

They ask, is this a dream?

Where is the ship we sailed upon (or flew in)?

Or was it simply a Netflix distraction?

But the unrelenting heat wakes them again, coming towards them at a speed that collapses time, burning down empires, furloughing minds, and melting net worth.

Everything in Mother's path becomes ash.

Adam rises, with their firstborn daughter swathed and cradled, and runs toward the sea, so thick with steam, hands cannot be seen in front of unbelieving eyes.

Teenager

I damn burst tears and say it, and I say it, and I say it.

I am pregnant. I am a fast girl. I am a harlot, unclean, used.

I am not a Virgin. I am not married.

I will not go backward.

Growing up without a map, no way to know where she'll land, thinks the mother.

Who says, 'I see a sunbeam has spilled through an unlocked window and filled your room like smoke.'

Dark Side of the Moon steadies the daughter, her face pushing past the teen door, her waxed wings melting in Mother's glare.

She throws her following sentence like a dart.

'I left a note for Daddy on the seat of his car.'

Mama says, 'Why didn't you tell me first?'

Papa

Daddy was a soft-throated man, a never fully-opened-throat-man. His lips would purse, almost like he was going to whistle, but would part just enough to let out a cartoon melody.

'Good morning, goo-ooo-od-morrrrnnnning, you slept the whole night through', singing our breakfast is ready and the sun is up.

He was singing in the rain; I was swimming back to shore.

Mama

The daughter asked if she had gone to heaven.

'We welcome her to the boneyard,' Mother replied.

And the daughter mouths *I love you* through tears held back so long they are dust, silent as a desert father.

Mother answered a question with a question; 'Are we beholden or enchanted?'

Habits become habitats. We have fallen. Fallen far away from the trees.

Yet a cunning monkey survives deep inside thee.

They both sense a rustling, a thicket of amber waves concealing two hungry eyes revealing a pattern.

Mother shouts to the unseen,

'How dare the world be other than what we've been told?'

Expectations

I dreamt my mother chewed a giant hole
through my back
desperate to become one with me.

She did not get what she came for.
Her rage became a gathering,
a slow crawl to the sea.

I did not expect to have empathy with her.

Judgement

Mama asks, 'Are you trying to grow out your hair again?
It won't look good long, so cut it short-short-short for
frizzy hair like ours. Wearing a wig in this weather is
easier. I keep mine under our bed.

'Let's order; I'm starving,' Mama says.

Liver and onions, liver and onions, liver and onions.

Eat bile, then weep, bile-weep, and the daughter
pours Mini Moo's into the blackness and says, 'Utah,
where I was born?'

'Where I grew strong, climbing, cartwheeling,
bicycling, and menstruating. Each spiral I made upward
reflected her little brother's downturn in your eyes,
Mommy. His muscles shrank, his spine contorted. His
body withered as mine blossomed, his inverted tree to my

kundalini rising ...'

Mother said, 'Remember when you wanted to be a nun? I had to remind you that we are not Catholic.'

Looking at her own saccharine tornado forming, she continued. 'Stop chewing your nails; you've bitten them to the nub. Who's going to want to put a ring on that hand? You'll end up marrying a truck driver.' She continued to stir.

'Mother, please, tell me where I was born and where he went underneath your mother's wing as I reached for the sun. I just wanted you to see me and celebrate my pleasure, which seemed to pinch against his bones.'

Mother looks up. 'I just want us to be friends. I never understood why you told your father first. He always said you've got hybrid vigour. And I just wanted you to stop doing "it."'

You were always bringing home exotic men.

Muzzy, muzzy, muzzy, her nose twitching like a cat. 'Eskimo kisses are best, and they won't get you pregnant,' she laughs.

The daughter's lungs are still inhaling brother dust. She looks out the cafe window through this layer of bacon grease just in time to see a red hawk open her wings and take flight; a little blackbird squealing in her craw.

Almost

My first visual memory is of a sparkler in the grass and a

beagle's nose.

Sulphur and fur, sensation becoming visual-fire on pink baby skin, whiskers trembling.

I remember stealing a pink quartz crystal from Johnny's diner. They were covering the pots of plastic green plants that separated one line of leatherette booths. Where did all the pink stones come from?

I was always getting lost on the way home from school. We moved around so much, but the neighbourhoods all looked the same to me.

So I left my little stone in front of our door to avoid accidentally walking into the wrong house and asking the wrong Mommy for a peanut butter and jelly sandwich.

My little brother came home after surgically having his Achilles tendon severed, having been away for two weeks while I watched a drunken nanny spank my toddler sister.

*

A schoolmate and my personal bully, Jill, is holding me underwater in her backyard swimming pool, and I begin to see the whole world going all kaleidoscopy. She releases me, and I cough all the way home, away from the sound of her giggling.

Sneaking out of my teenage bedroom window, I meet my best friend Mary, who taught me how to:

1. Ride horses English style; spurs are cruel

2. Lie to your mother when you require freedom

3. Lay together naked and kiss with tongue

Midwifery

Adam collapses into her arms; his mercury-winged calves are useless when there is no mountain to climb, no damsel to rescue. The daughter floats full of milk, nipple bursting in her mouth, boob raft.

And his arms around her neck as she breaststrokes further from the burning shore. A boat appears made of waste wood, crafted by gull tears and lost whale songs. Rickety is a word.

She begs him with her eyes, one armed with a daughter and the other extended towards a lover. Use your legs to climb upon us. The ark between them becomes a guiding star, and Adam takes the fruit of this offering so they can rest, drift in the mist, and dream-clean their nest.

Fever Dream

I am a bride, a royal bride, a virgin bride, a menopause'd bride.

I am wearing white. I am wearing starlight. I am wearing a glass filled with milk.

Beaded with antique lace, it was handed down by hands that swelled and cracked with overuse.

I am walking down the aisle. I am walking towards the queen.

She wears all the colours from all the places she has travelled to.

She wears rubies surrounded by clay. She wears emeralds polished by hollowed earth.

She wears pearls torn from oyster flesh, the scent of warm seas under her bosom.

Emeralds traded for landslides, turquoise alongside her dry eyes

Tourmaline is torn from mountains separated from rivers, now dry.

A limousine glides by holding the maiden bride, a pregnant bride whose hair rests in her lap twined around her henna-d hands.

A golden fawn brown, soft as corn silk, sweet as milk with roots caw-cawing raven black.

Racing down her backside, caressing her thigh side, shoulders, and cheeks along the roadside.

Her eggs travel inside, down womb tubes sliding into mouths opened bird-wide –

See how we fool death?

See how we spend our nine lives?

Next Life

I am a sleuth, a middle-aged femme fatale, and an abandoned mom parked outside a strip club. My freshly-tinted cover-the-grey paprika is wrapped in a cream-coloured scarf, contrasting my ebony cat-eyed sunglasses. I am elegant, a mystery-laden disguise. As my noon-day pupils dilate in dim, smoky light, I fumble for the apple wrapped in Kleenex at the bottom of my white leatherette in case I get hungry. My camera phone is on the ready.

My childhood desire to dress up, combined with voyeuristic tendencies, has come in handy; I am now spying on my daughter, Eve.

The plan is to find a corner table, wait for her to come on stage, and smartphone-click my way into an intervention.

Beautiful Eve, intelligent and athletic, gentle and daring – the phrase woman-girl comes to mind. It was she, even as a baby, who brought healing to my sad little heart as I patted her dry or warmed her bottle at 3 a.m. She turned my tears to laughter, my hunger for love ever sated.

Eve's tomboy girl body, lean and pale as a moonbeam, stepped on the micro-stage to share the spotlight with a shiny metal pole. She was barely covered in a black leather bikini, a weblike creation that made her look more like a superhero than a stripper.

Walk this way, the jukebox plays; Eve obliges and immediately pulls herself up and over, legs where arms should be like some holy multi-limbed goddess. I've always wondered where she got this kinaesthetic wisdom. She can climb a rock wall, smooth as an onyx, swim in glacier-melt lakes, or run long, hot miles without a single shade tree.

She pulls off her black velvet cap and releases all that furious hair. Her hair, my father's hair, is the colour of the sun through a dust storm. One in a hundred heads, locks of fire that burn the eyes right out of Moses. It lashes out, like water gushing onto black linoleum, polished thin from a thousand different bodies, all moving towards the not-allowed touch.

Men gather around, and I am further shielded from my daughter's eyes. Facing the sweat-stained and weary, cigarette-tinged fan hands offering coiled and beer-scented dollar bills. She doesn't seem to see anyone but is moving to some unseen reptilian realm.

I am mesmerised by the beauty of her current, the rage molting into desire, softening even the most puritanical part of me. I cease to be Mother; she is no longer Daughter.

Why did this ever offend me?

This sacred place, a cave wall encoded with spirals and unknown alphabets, an offering, an undulating prayer?

Departure

We arrived long ago, and I have lost memory of previous guests. But I always sensed a golden thread emanating between what was and what will be.

We are going home.

Breathing in the great rhythms of sunrise-sunset.

My space-mate sips his tea from the coffee mug we made with our wedding photo on it. He watches me exit this body like water moving downstream …

'Adam, please find me again,' I whisper.

I am an Earth mama metamorphosing, dissolving, and preparing to be reborn.

His touch fills my bones with code …

My eyes close, and a stone spiral staircase emerges, leading to an enormous blue sky; I want to see the view.

Some light has brightened my way, and my breathing loosens.

I hear birds and tiny leaves moving gently back and forth between the seasons – green to yellow, crimson now only bare branches.

Something in me quivers, a wave in my belly, a feeling of peace.

Eggs, beeswax, and frankincense, my hands reaching …

A ship with large, wind-filled, moon-shaped sails approaches me.

Bird, horse, turtle, dove, cat, cow, and snake a chorus.

My entire body vibrates, then opens, and I am

released from a pain that rises and becomes a great singing.

I look down and see a giant mountain bursting forth from between my legs, and Adam is on his knees, saying, 'Push, push, hold.'

Push, push, hold.

When You Miss Me I'm Gone
by Talisha McKnight

Chapter One

✔ Remember to breathe slowly and steadily

✔ Survey your surroundings to ensure you are not drifting

✔ Look out for sharp objects

✔ Make sure your gear is clean and ready to use

✘ Always dive with a buddy you trust

Floating face-down on the surface of the tranquil, turquoise waters, her still form appeared lifeless. The sun cast a shimmery glow onto her black wetsuit, creating rippling sparkles. With a swift flip of her fins, she resurfaced and hoisted herself out of the water onto the edge of the steep rock cliff. Not quite content with the venture of her quick dive, the diver lifted her mask and goggles from her face and swung her still-finned feet into the water. She had hoped to encounter more of the friendly but curious sea creatures, including stingrays and turtles, that usually used the spot as their playground. The scorching heat of the sun had now warmed the previously cool waters, transforming it from a refreshing oasis to a sauna. The ripples attracted a school of small wrasse fish that scattered back and forth, their blends of violet-purple scales cascading through the water.

Diving had become like meditation to her since moving to the tiny, secluded Belle Isle. It was a sudden change from her boarding school, and she was quickly learning to adapt. It didn't help that the reason for the change was because her parents were missing.

Six months, three days, two hours and fifteen minutes.

That's how long they had been gone. She still couldn't wrap her mind around how expert divers could go missing during a diving expedition. Her parents practically ate, slept, and breathed diving, and had meticulously trained her in the dos and don'ts of diving from birth. Everyone believed that they wouldn't find her parents. She did not believe this. Not only that, she knew her parents; they wouldn't just go missing during a dive.

A bright aura of lights dancing beneath the water distracted Tanisha's thoughts.

'What in the world?'

She parted her fins to confirm her sighting but was quickly disappointed. 'Hmm, I must be losing it.'

As it became less humid, a brisk breeze fluttered

through the air. Tanisha realised she must have spent more than an hour swimming and then sunbathing on the cliff near the water. It was best to start making her way back home to face her grandmother's wrath for once again evading her daily duties. Although she wasn't accustomed to completing a line of orders, her grandparents (mostly her grandmother) were firm believers in 'instilling a sense of duty' into their idle granddaughter.

Swiftly changing out of the wetsuit, she slipped into a dry tank top and shorts. She replaced her fins with slippers, which were more comfortable for walking, and decided to take the longer route home instead of her usual shortcut. No use rushing home to a lecture. The island, although small, was magnificently beautiful. Tanisha was in constant awe of the surrounding landscape and nature. Her parents never talked much about their home island, and whenever they did, she vividly remembered the uneasy glances they shared before shifting the conversation.

Why would an eleven-square-mile island with barely 1,000 people cause them that much discomfort? Or fear?

Tanisha's stroll took her from the dirt path leading away from the jagged cliffs onto perfectly-kept paved roads. Her walk should take ten minutes along this way, but she could easily stretch it to twenty. It wasn't long before the clearing of exquisitely green palm trees alongside the road led to the island's centre. It was a hotspot for tourists and locals alike.

Tanisha felt as if she had stepped into another world. The tall, modern buildings looked out of place next to the crystal-clear waters, swaying palms, trees, and cliffs that sat right behind it all. People with bright smiles, shades, tans, and swimsuits now walked along the stretch of plazas that lined both sides of the street. Maybe she would play her favourite roadside game to pass the time. Tanisha enjoyed deciphering whether the drivers of the cars riding through the affluent area were locals or tourists.

A black sedan, windows low, tail light missing, the driver (a bald man, in his fifties with a patchy beard) staring into the distance: local.

Bright green Jeep, no windows or any covering for that matter besides the railings and doors (for obvious safety reasons), packed with a mixed group of guys and girls that looked no older than their early twenties and with hair blowing in the wind, boasting signature honey-tanned skin: definitely tourists.

Red Mustang, windows rolled up, darkly tinted, music vibrating loud enough throughout its sleek exterior to earn dirty stares: local, probably a young guy, and strikingly handsome with a wide, white-toothed smile that could distract her long enough to almost get hit by a car!

The loud, extended blowing of this new character to the game, a Range Rover horn, dragged Tanisha from her thoughts and instantly reminded her of a rare category of drivers she despised: the privileged. At least that's what she called them, since their influence echoed through every inch, nook, and cranny of the island. The logo for 'The Party' – the sun with the name of the investment group that played a vital role in the development of practically everything on Belle Island – reflected from the back of the vehicle's windows. These were the people who flew out on private jets daily, cut ribbons for the opening of their countless hotels and private villas, managed the island's only research lab and factory, and only smiled for scheduled photo ops.

They owned the island, and never let the people forget it for a minute.

The darkly tinted window of the Range Rover rolled down slowly to reveal a perfectly dark, tanned face accentuated by a maroon shade of matte lipstick (that Tanisha vowed to find later), thick, equally arched eyebrows, and eyelashes that only the goddess of beauty could have gifted.

'Little girls must be careful when crossing the road,' the SUV's passenger said slowly, ensuring that each word that escaped her lips inflicted a sting. Tanisha inhaled and then exhaled to avoid responding. This was one time she would take her grandmother's advice and remain quiet. She had heard enough stories about the repercussions suffered by those who even slightly challenged anyone from the elite group.

'I'm sorry. I'll be more careful next time.' Just saying the words burned her. She rarely apologised. What was the use of apologising when the act had already been done?

'I understand. It must be so hard, especially with the recent update on your case.' Her grimace turned into a pretend, pitiful smile.

'What do you mean? My parents are still on a diving mission.' Her heart started to pound in her chest and she could feel the tears running to escape her eyes.

'Oh dear, to be young and foolish. It's best you run home now. Your grandmother has some news to share with you. Just know that we at The Party are here for you and your family during this tragedy.'

With tears streaming down her face and a flurry of panicked thoughts rushing through her mind, Tanisha decided, after all, to use her shortcut.

Chapter Two

Darla Taylor had lived on Belle Island her entire life. She was there when the island comprised only one school, a church, and a grocery store, and everyone old enough either worked in farming or fishing. She hardly recognised the island now and never ventured further than her house and farm near the island's edge. Many people tried to buy or even evict her from her land.

Darla was unwilling to part with her family home. She had grown up and raised her only daughter there until she left the island. Tanisha was her only grandchild. She had been worried but relieved when she came to live with her and Earlington – her husband – when Tanisha's parents were first declared missing. She had never met Tanisha in person, only via photos and phone calls. Her daughter had thought it best that Tanisha not visit Belle Island. Heartbroken, Darla and Earlington had accepted their daughter's decision.

The first day Tanisha stepped through the door, a flood of memories swept through Darla's mind. She was her mother's twin – average height, with broad shoulders to complement her plump frame. Her round face was set with two dimples, pouted lips, and a butterfly-shaped nose matched her small, dark brown eyes which glistened.

Today, however, her granddaughter had sweat dripping down her smooth, dark brown skin. Tanisha's afro puff, which she usually wore in a slicked-back bun, cascaded around her head like the sun's rays.

"Where have you been? I expected you hours ago. I understand what's happening, girl, but you can't disregard every task I give you,' her grandmother said.

'Is it true?' Tanisha asked with a tremble in her voice.

'What?'

'Is there news about my parents?' she said, trying to hold back tears.

'Wh–who told you that?' her grandmother asked in a hushed tone.

Frustrated with the lack of answers, Tanisha stomped her feet, causing water to fall from her hair onto the carpet. She dashed past her grandmother into the small room her grandparents had prepared for her six months ago when she arrived on the island. Tanisha had since added her drawings to the walls; sketches showing the crystal-clear turquoise waters that gave her solace when diving. Beneath the water, she had added clusters of Elkhorn coral that extended themselves like open palms, surrounded by beds of purple and yellow sea fans visited by a medium-sized stoplight parrotfish whose yellow spotted fin stood out like a traffic light. Sketching was a second refuge for her, a way to forget, if even for a moment.

Throwing herself on her bed, she buried her face in the pillow. Was it true? Had they found her parents' bodies?

Reaching under her pillow, she pulled her cell out and stared at the display screen. It was the last picture she had taken together with her mum and dad. She remembered the day clearly. They had taken a break from their diving and research to visit her for Parents' Day on campus. Once a month, the school invited families to spend time with their children. Her parents rarely made it, and she had become accustomed to hiding away in her room or the library on those days. That day, however, they had come and taken her out to lunch at a fancy restaurant. She remembered the menu was Caribbean-themed, inspired by various spicy and well-seasoned fish dishes, rice, soup, and other meat options, including oxtail, chicken, beef, and mutton. Her dad joked about this being her best meal since leaving home. She had always enjoyed her dad's sense of humour, cringy but still sweet. Her mum was quieter and more reserved – although she liked to keep up appearances for the outside world. That day, though, she was chatty, constantly asking questions about Tanisha's grades, friends, love interests (at which she awkwardly cringed), and plans. Tanisha's only goal at the time was to take a gap year to go on a diving expedition with her parents. She tried sharing the idea with them, but they responded cautiously.

'Tanisha, this isn't why we paid for you to get a quality education,' her mum retorted.

Her dad placed his hand reassuringly on her mom's. 'I have to agree with your mum on this one. It's not the life we want for you. And yes, I know we've taught you to dive, but it was just for fun. Diving professionally like us can be dangerous and less exciting than you think. Think it over for a bit, turtle, okay?'

Although he wanted to be empathetic, Tanisha knew this was the end of the conversation. She had agreed to rethink the diving gap year, but the opportunity never came around again to discuss the matter. Waiting for their meal to arrive, her dad took the chance to move out of his seat and gathered her and her mother into a bear hug, his six-foot frame towering over them. His goofiness was a mismatch to his burly size, and if people saw her parents standing side by side, they would imagine he was as stern as her mother was friendly. They would be wrong.

'Let's get a picture, for old times' sake!' her dad chirped.

Rolling her eyes, her mom set her phone into position with the timer on.

'Gerard, please avoid funny faces. We need a proper picture with Tanisha for the family album – and our socials,' she said with a smirk.

Her dad raised an eyebrow and responded, 'Now, Yvonne, why would I dream of ruining an excellent picture?'

'Mum, Dad, the timer is going to go off in three seconds!'

Tapping the screen, Tanisha smiled at the funny face her dad had made by pulling his ears and posing with a loopy grin while she and her mum looked at him – her exploding in laughter and her mum with a surprised open-mouthed smile.

Tanisha intended to remember them this way.

A loud knock on the front door pulled her from her reflection. She tiptoed to the door and pressed her ear against it. The only thing she could hear was murmuring and then sobbing. The door closed, and before Tanisha could step away, she heard her grandmother approaching her room.

No!

She would not open the door when her grandmother knocked. There was no knock.

'Tanisha, I know you don't want to hear it, but I'll be in the kitchen when you're ready.'

Would she ever be ready?

After sitting with her back against the door for what felt like hours, Tanisha stood up and headed to the kitchen. Her grandparents sat at the small table with solemn faces. Her grandmother stood and reached for her, wrapping her in a hug. She could smell her floral perfume; it was soothing.

'The police were here to say that they have exhausted their search for your parents.'

She felt the tears falling down her face, and this quickly turned into continuous sobbing.

Her grandfather moved his wife to her seat and lowered her into the chair.

'Tanisha, the police have changed the status of your parents' case from missing to being classified as a drowning. They have closed the case,' her grandfather said.

Her breathing quickened, and her heart felt like it would burst from her chest.

'I can't breathe – I can't breathe.'

Darkness shadowed her vision, and Tanisha collapsed onto the floor.

The Four Loves of Professor Waldman
by Emma Rogers

Chapter One
Ten Years Ago

As Professor of Anatomy at Ingolstadt University, Waldman spent most of his working life surrounded by death. As he observed his faculty colleagues, and listened to the Dean concluding his speech, he was blissfully unaware of how soon it would come knocking on his own door.

'So, may I formally present your new Vice Chancellor, Angela Krempe!'

Frau Krempe stood and waited for the applause to subside before speaking.

'Thank you. It gives me enormous pleasure to be voted into the role previously held by my beloved husband.' She paused, indicating the picture of Professor Krempe displayed at the front of the room. 'I know he would have been overwhelmed at the thought of having this wonderful library named after him. I would also like to thank all those involved in the restoration of this magnificent building, which as you know is one of the oldest in our university, and home to the original anatomy lecture hall. I'd particularly like to extend my gratitude to Professor Waldman for agreeing to chair the restoration committee.'

She scanned the room until she spotted his solitary figure at the back, partly obscured in the shadows. He reluctantly stepped forward and raised a hand in response to the ripple of applause, before retreating into the darkness once more.

'Now, I won't detain you any longer,' Frau Krempe continued, 'as I know you're all keen to enjoy the splendid buffet which has been provided for us next door ...' Laughter echoed around the room. 'But first a toast, to the University of Ingolstadt!'

'To the University of Ingolstadt!' the guests repeated, raising their glasses.

Some of Waldman's colleagues muttered their congratulations as they pushed past him, a few even shook his hand, but his attention had already drifted elsewhere. He gazed around what was now the Krempe Memorial Reference Library, contemplating the expanse of books that soared high into the air, and allowed himself a moment of pride.

Feeling sentimental, he breathed in the unique, musty aroma he always associated with a room full of old books. So much of his own history was bound up in this place; several generations of his family had studied within these walls, qualifying as physicians of one kind or another, and he was not the first Waldman to teach here. His ancestor had probably stood in this exact spot at some point during his tenure as Professor of Chemistry, over two hundred years ago.

Glancing towards the heavy glass doors at the entrance, it pained him to think they would be locked overnight, but he accepted it was necessary. Many of the books were rare and therefore valuable, but their monetary value didn't interest him, only the knowledge they contained.

Draining the last of his wine, he felt a hand on his elbow and turned to find Dr Henry Clerval standing beside him. 'So, what did you do to be burdened with that particular task?'

The question appeared simple, but the answer was complicated, and this was neither the time nor the place for such a personal explanation. Henry had once been his student, but Waldman now considered him a trusted friend, and respected him too much to avoid the question completely, or worse, lie; and so he settled on a half-truth.

'My motives are entirely selfish I'm afraid,' he said, and was touched when Henry raised a sceptical eyebrow, as if he were unable to believe him capable of selfishness.

He continued, 'Chairing the committee enables me to have a direct influence on the books housed within the library. I'm merely ensuring our students have access to the most comprehensive range of medical texts available.'

Henry cleared his throat, 'Trouble incoming,' he whispered, alerting Waldman to a figure weaving her way purposefully towards them, then stepped aside to allow the visitor to join them.

Angela Krempe smiled. 'Good evening, gentlemen – may I interrupt?'

'Of course. I'll see you when you get back from your trip, Professor.' Henry said, before wandering off towards the promised delights of the buffet.

'I know you're keen to leave promptly, but I wanted to catch you before you do so,' she said.

Unsure where the conversation was heading, he merely nodded, resisting the urge to check his watch.

'I understand you're leaving for Darmstadt first thing tomorrow?'

'That's correct.'

'And you're off to the emergency department this time?'

'Yes.'

'I know my husband never really understood the point of your – now how did he put it?' She tapped her lip with a finger, then arched an eyebrow. 'Excursions?'

He sighed inwardly, frustrated yet again at having to justify himself; surely how he decided to spend the summer recess was up to him? 'The point of my secondment is, firstly, to keep my own practical skills up to date. Secondly, to ensure my knowledge keeps pace with what is happening in acute medicine, thereby ensuring our curriculum is as relevant as possible for our students.' He paused, wondering, frankly, if there was any point to this conversation.

Frau Krempe studied him. 'Please, go on,' she encouraged, leaning forwards.

'Gaining this knowledge and experience also benefits our own hospital. By observing practices elsewhere, we can assess whether our own procedures could benefit from review. That is the *point* of it,' he concluded, failing to disguise the frustration in his voice.

Her smile was fleeting, 'Oh, I think you misunderstand me, Professor. I didn't mean that I agreed with my husband, quite the opposite in fact.'

He was momentarily thrown by her response. His relationship with Professor Krempe, both personal and professional, had not been easy and they disagreed often. He assumed Krempe's widow would simply pick up where he had left off.

'I do see their importance, which is why, if you are in agreement, I'd like to arrange some time for us to discuss your latest findings when you return.'

He remained silent whilst he considered what she'd said.

She smiled softly, 'I know you and my husband didn't see eye to eye on many issues, but he did respect you.'

He frowned; based on his experience of the man, that seemed unlikely.

'You don't believe me?' She lay a hand on his arm, 'Well, you'll just have to trust me on that.'

As she walked away, he stared after her. Perhaps,

finally, he had a Vice Chancellor who would be proactive and with whom he could collaborate. Something to mull over on the journey to Darmstadt.

One Week Later

Listed by Waldman as his next of kin, Henry was first to receive the news. Not that he was aware of the implication when his mobile phone rang as he stood in the Professor's faculty office, returning a book. Peering at the screen, he didn't recognise the number and declined the call.

'Thanks for the coffee, Catherine.'

'My pleasure Henry, it's always good to see you,' Waldman's personal assistant replied, clearing away the cafetière.

As a medical student over fifteen years earlier, he fondly recalled her supportive smile as he waited, chewing a fingernail, for his first tutorial.

His mobile rang again. He rolled his eyes and shrugged an apology in her direction, 'Henry Clerval speaking.'

The reason for the call from Darmstadt Hospital quickly became apparent, and a feeling of dread settled in the pit of his stomach as he listened.

'Okay, I understand,' he said eventually, glancing at Catherine, who was watching him intently. 'Yes, of course. I'll come straight away.' He ended the call and grabbed his bag.

'What's happened?' she asked, concerned.

'The professor … he's been stabbed.'

She clutched at the gold crucifix around her neck, 'What? Wh–?'

'They didn't elaborate. He's in surgery,' he said, keeping his tone deceptively neutral.

'Will he be alright?' she asked, her eyes filling with tears as she sank slowly into her chair.

He bit his lip and attempted a reassuring smile. 'I'm sure he'll be fine.'

'Will you keep me updated?'

'Of course. I need to go.'

His smile vanished as soon as he closed the door behind him.

*

Four hours later, Henry burst through the doors of the Darmstadt Hospital Emergency Room and headed straight for the reception desk.

'Professor Waldman? Where is he?' he demanded, noticing a police officer talking to a tearful nurse.

A doctor appeared, 'Dr Henry Clerval?'

'Yes.'

'Dr Richter, Trauma Consultant. We've just received confirmation that he's out of theatre. Follow me, I'll take you to the recovery suite.'

Henry breathed a sigh of relief; he'd steeled himself

for worse news.

'Professor Waldman sustained two abdominal stab wounds.' Richter held open the door for him and gestured to the lift. 'I was first to assess him. Luckily, we were able to respond quickly; any delay may have changed the outcome considerably.'

Henry simply nodded.

Once inside, Richter waited until the lift began its ascent before saying gently, 'We lost him for a few minutes.'

Nausea bubbled up from the pit of his stomach and he forced himself to breathe deeply.

'There was significant blood loss resulting in cardiac arrest,' Richter explained, 'but after successful resuscitation, he was sent for emergency surgery.'

Henry's mind was still racing when the lift halted and they stepped out onto the surgical floor. Richter introduced him to the Ward Clerk who indicated the waiting area. 'Take a seat. I'll let them know you're here.'

'I'm sorry, I have to get back; with the Professor out of action, we're one short downstairs,' Richter said, turning to leave.

'What do you mean?'

'We're waiting for another doctor to come in and cover the rest of the Professor's shift.'

His eyes widened. 'You mean this happened here?'

Richter pursed his lips, 'Yes. He was stabbed by a patient.'

Henry was rendered speechless; of all the scenarios he'd tormented himself with on the drive up here, he never envisioned this. *A patient? In the hospital?*

'Dr Clerval?'

He turned in the direction of the voice and merely nodded at the nurse now standing in front of him.

'Professor Waldman isn't awake yet, but I thought you'd like to see him.' She steered him down the corridor. 'I'm Staff Nurse O'Rourke, but please, call me Bernie. I'm on shift for the rest of the night.' She smiled kindly, 'I expect it's been rather a shock.'

'Yes,' he said, massaging his forehead.

Opening the door to Waldman's private room, she peered inside. 'Not sure how much longer it will be before he comes round but you're welcome to sit with him, as long as you don't mind me pottering about.'

He lingered in the doorway. It was quiet except for the regular beep of the ECG. Waldman was covered with a light blanket. A series of wires and probes connected him to the bedside monitoring equipment. Henry noticed him frown and his hand twitch. As the movement became more obvious, Waldman's facial expression became increasingly distressed; his jaw clenched and the muscles in his neck stiffened.

An alarm sounded and a flashing alert appeared on the screen.

'Wait here a moment, please,' Bernie said, glancing at the digital display; his blood pressure had increased, and his heart rate was rising. Systematically checking the various lead placements and lines running from the equipment to Waldman's body, she made a note on the chart and seemed satisfied all was well, but the Professor continued to appear restless.

Laying a hand gently on Waldman's forehead, she murmured in his ear. 'Easy now. Relax. Just breathe.'

Henry was reminded of his wife, Mary, soothing one of their children after a nightmare; her gestures so tender and soft.

She continued whispering the phrases until Waldman's movements slowed and he became still once more. The alarm ceased and the ECG returned to its normal rhythm.

'Just a dream, I think. Albeit a distressing one,' Bernie concluded with a sad smile.

'Is that common?' he asked, as she pulled a chair forward for him.

'Dreaming? It can be. I guess it's the mind's way of trying to make sense of what's happened, to break out of the fog of anaesthetic.' She shrugged. 'Well, that's what I think based on my experience.'

'Makes sense to me,' he said, wondering what the Professor would think of her theory.

'Given what happened to him … why he's here, perhaps it's not surprising that those dreams are a little more … troubled.' She patted Henry's shoulder, 'Don't worry, I'll be keeping a close eye on him.'

He smiled, grateful for her reassurance.

'How about a cup of tea?'

'I think I need a schnapps …'

Bernie chuckled, 'If only! Unfortunately …'

'Tea it is then, thank you,' he replied.

After she'd left, he stared at Waldman, becoming increasingly unnerved by his ghostly pale complexion. Focusing his attention on the steady rise and fall of his mentor's chest, he remembered him as he had been only last week, standing tall and self-assured, with his beard neatly trimmed and long hair reaching his shoulders. When the Professor was working, he wore it tied back at the nape of his neck. He chuckled to himself; when Waldman's hair was loose, if someone had given him a leather jacket to wear, he wouldn't have looked out of place at a rock concert or biker convention. However, he generally favoured a smarter style; usually a tailored jacket, shirt, and waistcoat, paired with dark trousers and brown brogues. Henry always felt slightly crumpled in comparison.

Now, he wore only a thin hospital gown, his hair matted and unkempt. It was a distressing change in appearance, making it seem as though all of Waldman's confidence and strength had evaporated.

Henry closed his eyes. The feeling of unease that had sat at the back of his mind now came to the fore; *I can't lose him.* He pushed the thought away, refusing to contemplate it further.

Bernie returned with a mug and set it down on the bedside cabinet.

'I need to make a few calls,' he said after taking several large mouthfuls of the steaming sweet tea, 'I won't be long.'

'No rush, take your time,' she smiled, indicating Waldman. 'He's not going anywhere.'

Henry cast a fearful glance towards the bed.

'He'll be fine.'

He nodded, steadied by the conviction in her voice, and left the room.

Bernie went to the nurse's station intending to update the patient information board, but she'd forgotten Waldman's chart. 'Jesus, Mary and Joseph,' she muttered to herself, 'you'd forget your head, Bernadette, if it wasn't screwed on,'

As she entered his room, she noticed Waldman stir. No longer agitated but drowsy, his movements were slow and lethargic. Sure enough, he was coming round. She sat in the chair beside him and watched as his eyes fluttered open, then closed. He breathed deeply and sighed; a frown wrinkled his forehead. She lay a hand on his shoulder. His eyes opened again. He seemed to struggle to focus for a moment, and squeezed them shut, before opening them again. His eyes roamed around the room, slowly taking in his surroundings, before settling on her.

She smiled, 'Professor? Can you hear me?'

He blinked a few times, attempting to reply. His

frown returned.

'It's okay, don't try to speak just yet. You were intubated before surgery. The tube has been removed, but your throat will be sore for a while. Would you like some water?'

He nodded, rubbing his neck.

She lifted a cup to his lips, 'Slowly,' she instructed.

He swallowed tentatively and winced, then drank a little more.

'Enough?' she asked.

He nodded again.

'My name is Bernie.' She consulted his chart. 'And you must be Professor Jacob Heinrich Waldman?'

The faint trace of a smile crossed his face.

'That's quite a mouthful!' she chuckled, before leaning in a little closer, 'I'm sure my colleagues will address you as Professor, and so will I, when it's appropriate. It's a title which deserves respect, and I expect you've worked bloody hard to get it. However, you're not here as Professor of Anatomy, you're here as my patient so, when it's just the two of us, I'd like to call you Jacob. Is that okay?'

The smile was again brief, but she caught it before it disappeared. He nodded.

'Jacob, do you know where you are?'

'Yes,' he replied, his voice hoarse.

'And … why you're here?' she asked gently.

He breathed in sharply and froze. His eyes darted

towards the door as his hand gripped the bedsheet, knuckles turning white.

'Jacob? It's alright. He's not here,' she said calmly, reaching for his hand. 'He's no longer in the hospital; he's been arrested. You're safe now. Okay?'

He hesitated, casting another glance at the door, then nodded.

'Okay.' She smiled. 'I need to complete your observations, now you're awake. You just relax alright?'

He exhaled slowly and closed his eyes, 'Yes, Bernie.'

She smiled to herself; she liked him already and knew they would muddle along just fine.

*

A little while later, Henry reappeared at the door. Bernie gave a thumbs up and mouthed, 'He's awake.'

He glanced up to the ceiling. *Thank God.*

Bernie bent low and murmured in Waldman's ear.

She beckoned him over, 'I'll leave you two alone for a little while whilst I go and update everyone.'

Henry walked around the end of the bed, summoning every ounce of positivity he could in the hope it would mask his apprehension. He was relieved to see the Professor had a little more colour in his cheeks.

Forcing a smile, he said, 'That was a bit of a close shave, sir.'

Waldman gave a weak smile in return, 'Too close.'

He couldn't wait any longer, whispering the question which had been plaguing him ever since he'd arrived, 'Sir, what the hell happened?'

Waldman looked away for a moment. When he turned back, confusion was etched into every line on his mentor's face, and the fear in his eyes was a sight that Henry would never forget.

Under Your Eyes
by Nora Kerezovic

Chapter One

Cecelia Kennedy sat, trancelike, staring at the man who had just lacerated her spirit with his sharp words. He looked like Stuart, her caring husband; the one who'd recently helped carry her father's coffin, the one who gets up in the middle of the night to take care of their baby, and assures her that she's the best thing about him. Now, he sounded and acted like a stranger. She regulated her breathing before speaking.

'Stuart, that's not true and it's unfair. I thought you'd be happy for me, I worked hard for this – think of the bigger picture – for us as a family. You're jealous.'

Cecelia watched as he shook his head and sat back to accommodate the weight of the words that fell on the airport cafe table in front of him. He glanced at her and then to their son, Daniel, who was gnawing on a teething toy, mesmerised by the terminal's Christmas tree. Stuart reached for some napkins. 'I've got it!' she said, leaning over to clean the baby's crimson cheeks and wipe the dribble from his chin. 'Who's the best little man in town? Daniel Kennedy!' she sang. Daniel laughed and did a little wriggle, his part of the routine. Cecelia stood up and kissed his head. 'Mama loves you, forever! I'm just going to get some sweeties. I'll see you on the plane,' she said, putting on her coat.

'We'll all go. Our flight gate will be opening soon,' Stuart said, pointing to the departures board.

'I need to be on my own now.'

'Cissy, don't be ridiculous, sit down – we'll talk.'

'No, you've said more than enough – I'll see you at the gate.' Cecelia walked off with conviction, pulling her carry-on case behind her.

Why did he have to pick a fight? Why couldn't he just say *congratulations, I love you, you're amazing?*

'How dare he say I put my work first,' she said, like a ventriloquist through tight lips and gritted teeth. In her fury, Cecelia grabbed some magazines off the stand in the newsagents. Flicking through the glossy publications was disappointing. There was nothing on offer that she hadn't read before. *New Year, New You! Yeah, yeah. We need to get Christmas out of the way first.* Leaning over to abandon them in a neat pile on the bottom shelf, she was interrupted by a middle-aged member of staff. 'I'll take them.' She held out her manicured hands and tilted her head, signalling *you should know better.*

'Thank you. I'm sorry. I don't mean to make more work for you,' she said, looking into the shop assistant's overly done Cleopatra eyes. Surrendering the magazines made her realise that it was easier to apologise to a complete stranger than to her husband. Navigating her way past other travellers who were shopping in Duty Free, wasn't easy. Her cabin suitcase was heavy.

I should have left it in the cafe with Stuart. Storming off with it did make a bold statement, though.

Cecelia's lingering anger made her hyperactive sweet tooth scream for attention. She picked up two packets of pear drops. Buy one, get one free. Without hesitation she opened a pack and popped a yellow sweet in her mouth. Swirling it round, she allowed the sugar to gently scratch her tongue.

'Cecelia … Cecelia Jayne Kennedy, is it you?'

She looked at the tall airport security guard who was standing in front of her, baffled at how he knew her name and concerned that she was going to be accused of shoplifting.

'Cecelia … is it you?'

'Yes, yes, it is!' she said, pushing the sweet to the side of her mouth.

Before attempting to declare her innocence, he spoke again.

'You don't recognise me, do you? It's been over a year.'

No I don't. Think, think, think! No name badge, help! But I know his voice … she stood back to get some perspective. His unnaturally dark raven hair, rosacea and thick, dark rimmed glasses did not look remotely familiar to her. Nothing. All he offered was an awkward smile and an embarrassing silence.

'I escorted you to the hospital … you were in labour …'

'Harry! No way? Oh my good God, look at you! You've changed. You've really changed. Where's the beard? And you were …'

'Bigger!' he nodded, with an element of pride.

'I was going to say broader!' They both laughed. 'Your uniform threw me as well. Displacement and baby brain. Hey – I've transformed a lot since then too! Lost about three stone!'

'In your case due to a baby; Master Daniel. For me, it was combatting years of comfort eating. I'm a new man now!'

'You certainly are! Well done, Harry. Please don't judge me for eating these!' she said, holding up the bags of pear drops.

'I'd never do that. Not a woman with your exquisite taste. I was very impressed by the thank-you hamper you'd sent. Wherever did you find that hardback copy of *The Picture of Dorian Gray*?'

Internet shopping, that's where Stuart found it – he knows you better than me …

'Oh, in a quaint, second-hand bookstore in The Lanes, in Brighton.' The lie would have rolled off her tongue if she hadn't been sucking on the boiled sweet.

'How long have you worked at Heathrow? It makes a change from the newspaper, eh? Stuart didn't tell me you'd left the editorial team.'

'I am still in the newsroom. I'm here part-time, it was important for me to work in airport security, especially after editing a feature on human trafficking.'

A couple of teenage boys carrying snowboards asked to be excused as they shuffled past them, shopping for confectionery. Harry scowled.

'Those boards should have been put through in oversize baggage,' he tutted.

'Well, it was great to see you, Harry, it really was. Have a beautiful Christmas. I might see you at the office in the new year. I'd better go. I'm meeting Stuart and Little Boy Blue at the gate. My plane boards soon …'

'Gate twenty four? Aer Lingus EI267?'

'Yes, wow, you really know your stuff!'

'I do. It's a twenty-five-minute walk from here to that gate. You're aware of that?'

No, actually, I'm not. Even though I did the journey every month to see him … to spend precious time with him … Stop! Don't go there. Focus. No time for tears.

'I can get you there in less than seven minutes,' he pointed to an airport caddy outside the shop.

Absolutely, yes, I have a lot of apologising to do.

'Yes please. That would be great.'

'Come on,' he picked up her suitcase and strode towards the vehicle. She followed.

'I've always wanted to get into one of these. Stuart says they are either for grannies or gangsters,' she laughed.

He didn't seem to hear her. He beeped passengers out of the way.

'Too much congestion here. I'm going to take a short cut, through gates thirteen to twenty. They're under renovation. It will be like a ghost town.'

'Sounds good, thank you so much. I think it's fair to say you are my hero! Second time to the rescue.'

He smiled, turning the caddy towards gate thirteen. The digital clock on the flight panel displayed 12.34 pm. 'I'm just going to call Stuart, tell him I'm on my way.'

'No, don't do that!' He covered her handbag with his left hand. 'If they see you have a phone, I will have to answer to them.'

'Harry, relax, there's no one here. Why wouldn't I have a phone?'

'We are on CCTV. I'm only permitted to drive the frail, elderly or disabled. And you are not in any of those categories. We'll be there in two minutes. Think of the surprise Stuart is going to get seeing us.'

'Not all disabilities are visible, Harry,' she said, pulling her handbag nearer so that it sat under her elbow. He drove faster, past yellow ladders and scaffolding that had sheets of polythene hiding the fresh paintwork.

'Over there, to the left, is going to be a children's soft play zone. They've started on the mosaic. It's going be great – have a look.' She turned her head to see the formation of a glittery rainbow on the wall.

The blow to her carotid artery was swift and

successful. The caddy came to a halt. He took a firm grasp of her right arm as she slid sideways. The pear drops that she hadn't paid for were scattered on the floor of the cart. He propped her over the dashboard, flicking the syringe twice before injecting the liquid into her porcelain neck, behind her right earlobe. He brushed the sugar from the sweets from her beige cashmere coat. Smiling, he stroked her defined cheekbones with his sweaty fingers. Cecelia lay limp beside him. Asleep. Beautiful. His.

Chapter Two

The familiar scent of fresh tiger lilies was strong, encouraging her to wake up. Her eyes, like heavy doors, opened slowly and were drawn to the wild orange and magenta hues of the flowers. *Beautiful.* A plastic jug of water and a polystyrene cup stood on a pine nightstand. Her vision slipped in and out of focus. *Hospital. I'm in hospital.* Then two words made their way through the mental haze: *accident … airport.*

Sleep snuck up on her again and dragged her down to a deeper level.

*

Cecelia didn't sense when a fleece blanket was being placed on top of her duvet. She didn't feel when her clammy forehead was being kissed. She didn't hear the deep voice as he whispered a lie into her ear, 'You're safe now. I'll look after you.'

*

Palpitations ran through her and she woke with a jolt akin to someone who'd suffered an electric shock: stunned, hot and breathless. Her arms were tingling with pins and needles. With immense effort she managed to push herself up to a seated position. She tried kicking off the duvet, but her legs were powerless.

Have I had surgery? Her paralysed muscles reminded her how she'd felt the night Daniel was born. Her left hand pinched the bed covers and tugged them off.

No surgical gown. Was that the voice of fear or reason?

She was dressed in her own clothes. The outfit she'd chosen for their trip to Ireland. Black jeans and pale pink jumper, Stuart's socks, as always.

Panic slid over her numb body as she rapidly scanned the dimly-lit room.

Above her head was a slanted ceiling. *Loft room.* She surveyed the area … a white wardrobe, beige sofa, white table with two chairs, a pine rocking chair, oatmeal carpet, glass-panelled wall. Trees. Countryside. Then her eyes fixed on the door. Heavy. Three locks. Top, middle, bottom.

You're not in hospital, but you have been drugged.

Where am I? Where's Stuart? Where's Daniel? Gooseflesh stood to attention all over her body and she began shivering. Her instincts wanted her to call for help, but she'd lost control of the muscles in her jaw.

When she could no longer hear the percussion player pounding on her heart, she reached for a cup of water, sipping it cautiously. Was it just water?

The room was whirling. Her head hurt. Her body was numb. *Focus.* When her feet touched the carpet, she stood up. The floor ebbed and flowed. It reminded her of the first time she'd been intoxicated. It was December ... twenty years ago. She'd had the flu. Her father had made her a hot whiskey. It tasted vile but she trusted him when he said, 'This will knock that dose from here to kingdom come!'

Her vision started speckling. Static. No signal in her brain.

Don't faint. Sit. 'Too much, too soon!' That's what the midwife said when Cecelia fainted and caused herself a concussion. She recalled pleading in the maternity ward, 'I just want to go home.'

A serpent of nausea wriggled out of her stomach and up her throat. She began vomiting, loud and aggressive. Sobbing, she managed to call out, 'Help me! *Please*, help me!'

More vomiting. The door opened.

'Harry… Thank God. I … I … Please help me.'

'Cecelia, I'm not Harry. In this house, I'm Malcolm.'

What?

Holding up both hands, to prove he was unarmed, he advanced. 'Cecelia, I'm not going to hurt you.'

She put her right hand to her mouth and her left hand up to signal 'keep away.' 'Where am I? Where's Stuart and my baby?'

He looked at her and then to the puddle of nausea by her feet.

'I don't know. However, I can assure you that you're safe here. I will take great care of you.'

No! No! No!

'Harry, what are you talking about? I really don't understand, I need a doctor ... help me!'

'Malcolm. I'm Malcolm. There is no Harry here.'

Lunge for the vase ... throw it, hit him, run. Now!

Her legs buckled and her forehead hit the nightstand. Darkness. Too much, too soon.

Chapter Three

Wrong, it was all wrong. In the hundreds of thousands of words in Stuart Kennedy's vast vocabulary, *wrong* was the only word that fit.

He'd been waiting in the police station for nearly an hour. Pacing the room. Perching on the edge of the wooden bench and then sitting back in an attempt to get comfortable. Springing to his feet, he glanced into the pushchair often, checking on Daniel. Still sleeping, good. He hadn't wanted to take his son to the police station. That was wrong. He hadn't wanted to leave him at home with the nanny. Under the circumstances that felt wrong.

His trained eyes read every poster and leaflet on the notice board. Ignoring the Christmas decorations and fairy lights. Studying two photographs of missing people. Teenage girls. Disappeared. Wrong. He tried inhaling deeply, to accept the fact that Cecelia's face would be on a poster, but his lungs couldn't lift the anguish that weighed on his chest.

Tucking Daniel's feet under the fleece blanket made him miss her more. Cissy had a thing about cold feet. He remembered her telling him how Hans Christian Anderson's *The Little Match Girl* always made her cry. Her frozen feet, hunger and a heavy heart. He used to tease Cecelia for being so sentimental. Now Stuart could see it for what it was – compassion.

Daniel's cheeks were cherry red and swollen. In an echo chamber of memory Stuart could hear Cecelia's voice, 'Nasty teethy-toothies,' she'd said, the first time Daniel was teething. Remembering her gently applying teething gel to the baby's gums, with the pad of her little finger; rocking him in her arms, pacing the floor, willing his pain away, then taking him into their bed and singing to him until he settled and slept – that's love.

Stuart closed his eyes to watch the memory, to hear her sing … 'I'll tell me ma, when I go home the boys won't leave the girls alone, they pulled my hair and stole my comb, but that's alright 'til I go home …' Entranced by the memory, he whispered the chorus … 'She is handsome, she is pretty, she is the Belle from Dublin City.'

Tears, complete strangers to him, clouded his vision. He closed his eyes and allowed his head to rest against the wall, trying to consolidate his thoughts. Cecelia wasn't dead. He knew it. He *felt* it.

'Stuart, thanks for coming in. Sorry to have kept you waiting,' a short man said, flicking snow off his puffer coat and undoing his scarf. 'I'm DC Russell Bendelow, we spoke last night. This is Trainee Detective Julie Middleton.'

Stuart stood up, then shook their cold, damp hands. They didn't look like he'd imagined. They were dressed in dark suits and office footwear. No zest, no flair, no character. Not like Cecelia. Julie Middleton didn't seem like a name for a detective. Her hair was mousey brown and pinned off her face with one single clip. Old fashioned. Or was he being too judgemental? Maybe in their line of business it was best not to stand out.

They assured him that the WPC at reception would call him if Daniel woke. Stuart shook his head. *No.* In a firm yet polite tone, he said he was not letting his son out of his sight.

'Of course, if you feel that's best – this room is fine,' Julie said, gesturing to a door at the end of the corridor.

Stuart left the pushchair at the back of the room, then took a seat to join the people he hoped would be able to find his wife.

Aside from the table, three chairs and one window, the room had nothing else to offer. An interview space, the fewer distractions the better he thought. It stank. What was the smell that cheap air freshener failed to mask? Fear. He thought of asking them to open the window, but then changed his mind. It was freezing outside and he didn't want to appear difficult. They offered him a drink. He declined. Time wasn't waiting. It had been three whole days since he had seen or heard from Cecelia. He was keen to start the interview.

Russell leafed over some sheets of paper then placed a recent photograph of Cecelia on the table. Her black and white professional head shot from her workplace, *Joie de Vivre*. Classic and beautiful. Stuart remembered the day it had been taken – the same week she'd been promoted to Creative Director.

The questioning began. Stuart knew the drill. Warm up questions first, maybe crack a joke, try to find some common ground, then time to dig into the grit. Interviewing was part of his profession, too.

The questions came in swift succession. He answered as best he could. Julie took notes. He was aware that she was more interested in reading his actions than recording his words.

It was surreal and nightmare-like, watching himself

go through the interview that was turning into an interrogation. His brain kept reality at a distance. As if it wasn't his wife, the mother of his child. This kind of thing only happens to other people. Not to him. Not to her. *Not to us.*

'I have all the police reports, Stuart. So, let's get this straight,' Russell said, holding both hands parallel as if he were directing traffic. 'You boarded an Aer Lingus plane, flight EI267, with your son, Daniel, from Heathrow to Dublin, on the 19th of December at 1.15 pm, without your wife, Cecelia.'

'Yes. That's correct. I did.'

'And you say, or at least you said it here when the police spoke to you on the 19th, that you didn't realise that your wife was missing? Even though you had an empty seat beside you on the plane?' Russell leaned in closer.

'Yes ... I did. But, Detective, it wasn't like that ...'

'What was it like, Stuart? Tell me, exactly, what was it like?'

Stuart's eyes were stinging from tears and exhaustion. Burying his head in his hands, he took time choosing his words.

'We had an argument. Cecelia was upset. She left me, us. She left us at the cafe.'

'By us, you mean you and the baby?'

'Yes.'

'I see. So when the cabin crew and the captain of the aircraft asked you what you wanted to do when Cecelia

hadn't boarded, you said ... "We can go without her".
Why? Why were you so insistent that they could? You
didn't think this was odd? You didn't think to call her? To
raise the alarm then?'

'No, I didn't think it was odd. We had an argument.
A fight. She stormed off, she takes a while to calm down.
She didn't answer any of my calls. I was trying to settle
Daniel, I just thought she'd get the next flight to Dublin
...'

His words hung in the air like onyx clouds.

'What was the argument about?'

'Stupid stuff.'

'Stupid stuff, I see – we're listening ...'

Recording. Judging. Convicting.

'Stupid stuff that couples fight about, Detective, like
... trying to get work-life balance.'

'So you're saying it wasn't balanced? Who tilted the
scales?'

'Yes. I'm saying it wasn't at all balanced. No one
tilted the scales ... we were just trying to find our feet.
Cissy had gone back to work. Grieving ... She'd lost her
dad. It was a seismic loss for her. She immersed herself in
that place and got a promotion. Long hours. Late nights.
A one-year-old. It's not easy. It wasn't easy. It was
unhealthy. I felt Cecelia put her work first. It was the be-
all and end-all.'

'Interesting. Wasn't easy for whom? For Cecelia, or
for you? She has a very generous salary, great benefits,

clearly she's good at her job. Successful woman. I understand your nanny, Sophy Hoen, lives in? That must have helped to make things easy? Not many couples can afford to have a child in nursery *and* live-in childcare.'

'This has nothing to do with money or Sophy, Detective. My wife is missing and *this* is the route you take?'

Stuart closed his eyes, sat back, regretting the critical tone he'd used.

'Stuart, I will take all the routes necessary to understand how you did not realise your wife was missing, when she didn't turn up at the departure gate. And how – ten minutes after your plane was in the air – a call was made to Scotland Yard saying that a bomb had been planted in Heathrow airport.'

His face became warm. Not good. 'Are you …? Do you …? Do you actually think Cecelia going missing has anything to do with a bomb scare?'

No answer. His frustration was mounting.

'Tell us why you boarded the aircraft without her.'

'I've told you. I boarded the plane because I thought she'd come later. It was a trip to *her* family. For her father's anniversary mass and a christening, she was going to be the godmother! She wasn't going to miss that!'

'So, when the cabin crew asked you if you wanted to get off the plane you said, and I quote, "No, I'm not going through all of this again!" What did you mean?'

Stuart drank the glass of water that was in front of

him, then poured another.

'I've explained this already. I meant I wasn't going to go through all the stress. Everything all over again, with the baby. Do you understand?'

No answer. The unspoken rule was loud in his ears – *you are not the person who is asking the questions.*

'Let me reiterate, I thought Cecelia would join us in Dublin.' Saying it out loud made it sound wrong. Very wrong.

The Detective and Julie said nothing as they reviewed their notes and documents. Stuart was compelled to speak again, to chisel into the block of silence.

'Cecelia wasn't with me on the plane, but I didn't know that she was "missing", in police terms, at that point.'

Russell looked at Julie then back at Stuart. He inhaled deeply and took his time before speaking. 'Explain to me the definition of missing in non-police terms.'

Leaning in closer, Stuart answered, 'In non-police terms, missing means lost or mislaid. Cecelia is not lost or mislaid, Detective Bendelow. She's been taken.'

The Death Spell of Solari
by George Wallace

Chapter One

Deborah knelt by the corpse to finish the embalming that would preserve the body, then applied cosmetics to the face to give the impression of life. She replaced the eyes with the eggs of a great crested hen, small enough to fit into the socket and which, when painted, made the person look alive. Her hands were shaking with exhaustion.

'Are you nearly finished?' Gyfard asked.

'Nearly,' Deborah said. Looking up and smiling at Gyfard, her mind went back to her parents and how she had adopted Gyfard as her grandfather. He suited the role perfectly, an oldish man about fifty-five with a small well-trimmed beard. He was perfect as a grandad, knew the right thing to say always and kept her on the straight and narrow.

Deborah adjusted Alfred's arms and legs. After all of her work, the dead body really could pass for a living one, dressed in his best clothes and shoes.

Deborah sighed. There had been so many deaths since the plague had arrived. The fog had appeared first; it just hung over the castle, making everything damp. It was followed by the storms, which blasted the atmosphere, but had no effect on the fog. Then people started dying: the only sign a big swollen lymph node.

The learned doctors checked out the bodies and proclaimed a plague. King Rycharde had ordered everybody embalmed and the scale of the work was killing Deborah and her team.

At last, Alfred was finished. Gyfard helped to move the corpse from the table to the coffin, then carefully arranged the clothing and the limbs. Deborah watched while Gyfard closed the lid and the assistants nailed it down before moving the coffin to its final resting place. Another one done.

Leaning on the embalming table, Deborah wiped the sweat from her eyes, her hand shaking with exhaustion. 'How many more today?'

'Six.' Gyfard avoided her eyes as she groaned. 'I know, but the plague has claimed so many.'

Deborah stretched her aching shoulders and gazed around the crypt for the thousandth time – she knew every brick, every table, every inch of the seven-foot walls. It smelled of dust and embalming fluid and, despite her efforts, of rot and decay. 'We've barely been outside in weeks,' she said. 'This is unrelenting; we can't even keep the coffins together in family groups any more.'

'The family groups stopped a while ago,' Gyfard replied. 'It's been almost impossible to keep up.'

'Gyfard, let's get out of this crypt. I've had enough for today, the last six can wait until the morning,' Deborah said.

'I agree.' He smiled.

'Let's eat. I'm starving and need to eat,' Deborah said.

They staggered up the stairs from the crypt and walked along the corridor towards the banqueting hall. A noblewoman walked past Deborah. *Look at her, beautifully made up, perfect face, beautiful clothes, while here I am with a bare face and dressed in rags. Why can't I look like that? One day it will be me*, thought Deborah, with a tentative smile to herself.

'Hang on a minute, Gyfard,' Deborah said, stopping to see her reflection in a window. Pale and hollow-cheeked, she looked far more mature than her nineteen years. Her face was framed by close-cropped hair – kept short for practicality – as dark as the inner crypt itself. She ran her finger down the scar that ran from ear to her chin, a gift from the man who murdered her parents. No point in worrying about him now, not with the plague. He was more than likely lying dead somewhere, or perhaps he had already been embalmed. She smiled at herself, showing perfect teeth and healthy gums.

'You should smile more,' said Gyfard, making her jump. 'You have a beautiful smile.'

'Not much call for smiling nowadays,' replied Deborah. She looked away from the window, towards Gyfard.

'One day I'll be dressed like that noblewoman, my scar hidden by makeup. Then, I'll smile all the time.'

Gyfard snorted. 'You wouldn't look like that, my little princess. You stay away from those daft court fashions, at least in this castle.'

They made their way to the banqueting hall. 'It'll just be the usual – bread, water, chicken, vegetables.' Gyfard nodded. 'It'll stick to your ribs though. The things you are guaranteed here are a roaring fire, clean tables and the servers.'

'The servers work very hard keeping the place clean, and we are all in this together to end this fog, the storms and this plague,' said Deborah, as they took a seat. 'Look at the top table for visiting royalty, it's always immaculate.'

'I much prefer eating all together – it makes the place more homely. Better than when we were all separated into different areas. Plus, everyone talks to one another now,' Gyfard said. 'Even although they are all terrified of the plague. Hopefully one day they'll find the cause and remove all these unknowns.'

'I agree, it's much better being together. It used to be terrible before,' Deborah said.

Their food was served. They were about to start eating when a woman walked past and everyone, except Deborah, turned to look.

'Stop staring at Lady Emelina, Gyfard,' she sighed. 'You men are all the same.'

He blushed. 'But she is so stunning. Almost married the prince, you know. Look at the way her long black hair frames her beautiful face. With that lovely black matching cloak.'

Their conversation was interrupted by a clap of thunder. The effect on the dining hall was varied, some screamed, a few put their head in their hands, some dropped food, and others ignored it.

'Another hour of thunder and lightning,' Gyfard said.

'Everyone is so used to the storms now, after the first clap of thunder,' said Deborah.

Gyfard shook his head. 'This is getting worse. Every night the same thing. The fog is bad enough. It gets everything damp – it's a thick veil of grey. The lack of sunlight means we're not getting our goodness from the sun. Something *must* end all of this and get us back to normal.'

'The bodies we're embalming are arriving in worse and worse condition. You're right.'

A woman two tables away started screaming, '*Stop!* Do you hear me? Go away! I can't stand this any more.' Two servers attended to the lady, putting an arm around her to calm her. Gradually, the sobbing subsided.

Deborah took his hand. 'I just wonder what caused all these things to happen all at once. It used to be great here. Now it's a terrible place to live. Do you remember we used to have visitors, bringing goods from all over? Now they can't get past the drawbridge.'

'At least we have our greens.' Gyfard looked rueful as he stuck a piece of broccoli into his mouth. 'My mum would be proud of me eating my greens.'

'Just eat your stale bread and drink your water,' laughed Deborah.

Before Gyfard could reply, there was a commotion in the entranceway to the banqueting hall. Shouts were ringing out, 'The Queen's Mother is dead! Long live the King!'

Deborah looked horrified at this news. *How am I going to cope?* she asked herself silently.

Gyfard said, 'The first of the royal family to fall.'

'How will we deal with the lying in state?' Deborah swallowed. 'We have six more to do from today alone.'

Gyfard sighed. 'We'll have to go back to the crypt – the Queen Mother comes first, the other six will have to wait. We'll manage.' He patted her hand.

'No, I want to get them out of the way,' said Deborah.

Men and women were running into the banqueting hall in tears. One woman, her motherly face drawn into lines of grief, ran up to Deborah and Gyfard's table. 'There you are! They're looking for you. They'll be bringing the Queen Mother to the crypt soon for the embalming.'

The hall was falling quiet and Deborah looked up. To her surprise, the lady Emelina was watching her, dark eyes narrowed with thought. As their eyes met, the lady blinked and looked away.

No one was eating any more; tears fell onto plates, and loud talk had turned into quiet murmurs that

Deborah could barely hear over the pounding rain, which battered the windows as if the sky itself was sobbing.

Deborah pocketed the heel of bread remaining on her plate and stood. As she followed Gyfard to the door, one of the old king's servants bowled into her. She had once been fat, but now, like everyone else, her flesh hung from her bones as if melted and her eyes were sunk into tired blackness.

Deborah caught her arm to steady her and the servant looked up. Her face was wet, her eyes red, and snot was running from her nose. 'Remember!' she said, putting her lips close to Deborah's. 'Remember, *he* is not the real king. *He* locked our king and queen away, cast a spell on them. Forced the elders to accept the adviser Rycharde as regent until the prince could be found. There is no legitimacy now. No-one left of the real royal family. None!' She spat with the vehemency of her words. 'Where is Terrance and his quiet friend who says nothing? The Queen Mother has died and they are nowhere to be seen.'

Gyfard pulled her away from Deborah. 'Don't speak like that where people can hear you! You want to disappear? They think you're harmless, but they won't if you can't shut up.'

Deborah blinked. 'Is what she said true? Gyfard?' She spun to look at him.

Gyfard forced a smile. 'Of course not. Rycharde is our rightful regent, named king by the elders. Don't you go thinking otherwise.'

Deborah looked back at the old woman who pulled her arm away from Gyfard's grip and staggered into the dining hall. 'No legitimacy,' she muttered. 'Not the real king. Where is the prince?'

To Deborah's surprise, it was Emelina who stood. She hurried across the room, her long skirts and cloak sweeping the stone floor. 'Come on, Auntie,' she said, putting an arm around the old woman. 'We all know how much you loved the Queen Mother, come and sit and have something to drink.'

Once more the old woman caught Deborah's eye and something hung in the air between them, until Gyfard gave her a nudge. 'Back to work, my dear,' he said.

*

Deborah sat alone in the crypt. Her fingers ached; her muscles screamed. Six embalmed, and all to the best of her ability. She hadn't cut corners even on the last one, when her knees were bruised from kneeling and her eyes burned from examining the details. Every corpse that came to Deborah would have the best of her, from Queen Mother to gardener's assistant. By now everyone had gathered in the banqueting hall to mourn and she had sent Gyfard to join them and then to go for embalming supplies as they were getting low. Now it was so quiet you could hear a pin drop.

Deborah tried to relax, dropping her shoulders to let the tension fall away. This was a strange place to feel happy, Deborah knew, but surrounded by the dead she had always felt tranquil.

Deborah crossed her arms and sank into her chair. Her eyes closed, and she was drifting towards sleep when she heard a noise, it sounded like flapping. *Must be a rat,* thought Deborah. Then, *wait! Rats don't have wings.* The sound stopped and Deborah relaxed again. *It's nothing,* she thought. Then the noise restarted. With a deep sigh, she got up to investigate. *The noise is not coming from here. It's coming from the Royal Crypt – and no one is in there except kings and queens who have passed away.*

Deborah crept to the doorway of the Royal Crypt and listened. The flapping was definitely coming from in there. She turned the handle slowly as the flapping continued. She cracked open the door and the flapping grew louder. *What could be behind the portal?* All sorts of witches, dwarfs and devils came into her mind. *Empty your mind,* thought Deborah, *your imagination has the habit of running wild, stop it.* When the door was open far enough to see in, Deborah peered around. There didn't seem to be anything inside the crypt. She strode forward, frowning. Was the noise all in her imagination?

Then she saw it: a bird the size of a sparrow and the colour of the sky on a clear day was sitting on a tomb. As Deborah drew closer, she could see the feathers and the metal on its body. The twinkle of its eyes told her it was a toy. She stared at the bird. Had it been forgotten in a royal pocket? It had to be valuable. Then she remembered that any theft was punishable by death. If someone found the bird in here, in the Royal Crypt, instead of in the nursery where it surely belonged, would she be blamed? Punished? Sudden fear made her look around, half expecting to see a royal guard in the doorway behind her, but she was alone, and all she could hear was the flapping of the wings.

'Come here, you!' whispered Deborah, and the bird hopped just out of reach. She dodged around a coffin and tiptoed towards the bird as if it was a living creature. Dashing after the toy, she caught it up and reached out to grab it, but it spread its wings, fluttered and flew just beyond her fingertips. Deborah gasped as it hopped onto a coffin. Shaking her head, she clambered up after it, her skirt trailing in the dust. Silently, she apologised to the royal dead as she followed it onto the next sarcophagus, trying not to think about the blasphemy she had to be committing. She jumped after the bird again and once more it flew just out of reach.

Deborah stopped. *This is ridiculous. This is a toy. There has to be a way to make the bird come to me.*

Thinking of the ladies she'd seen walking in the royal garden, she put out her left arm and extended her index finger. The bird stopped where it was and looked at Deborah with its twinkling eyes, then it cocked its head to one side. It flapped its wings and flew twice around her head, then it descended to land on her finger. Deborah gasped; the bird was so light; it had clearly been made by a craftsman who cared about their work. The feet, although metal, felt real. She stroked the feathers and found them soft as down. She brought the bird closer. She could see where the feathers had been inserted into the metal body. The eyes shone like diamonds. The bird closed its wings and settled on Deborah's finger.

At that moment, the crypt door opened and she jumped.

'I'm back!'

'Gyfard!' Without thinking, Deborah slipped the toy bird into her pocket. Much to her relief it lay still and did not flap or try to escape.

'I noticed we were low on supplies. Where do you want them?' His arms were full of bandages made from ripped linen, pots of herbs and jars of oils.

'In the corner, please.' Deborah was fighting for composure. Should she tell Gyfard about the bird? What if she was caught with it in her pocket? He could not be implicated. She patted her skirt and swallowed. She would have to keep it a secret until she could put it back, somehow, where it belonged.

'The final embalming will have an audience,' Gyfard said. 'And not the usual mice.'

Before Deborah could answer, the crypt door opened again and two servants entered carrying the Queen Mother's body on a stretcher.

'Where do you want Her Majesty, Mistress?' asked the first servant.

'On the table there, please.' Deborah pointed, very aware of the bird in her pocket. What if it started flapping now?

The servants lowered the stretcher onto the table, and gently moved the Queen Mother across to lie in the same place as every other corpse that passed Deborah's way.

With no choice, she concentrated on her task. The Queen Mother had always been a small lady but, in the end, she had lost weight like everyone else and looked very thin. She had been brought to Deborah in her night clothes and the expression on her face was peaceful.

'She died in her sleep?' Deborah whispered, and one of the servants nodded.

'Yes, Mistress.' Both turned to face the body, bowed deeply, and then left, carrying the stretcher with them.

Gyfard bowed himself, then he looked at Deborah. 'You look exhausted. Why don't you go back to our room to prepare yourself. I'll wait for the release of the fluids and let you know when you can start the initial embalming.'

Deborah smiled gratefully and returned to their room, continually checking on the bird in her pocket. It seemed to be asleep – it was so still it had become a living creature in her mind. She shut the door behind her and locked it, making sure Gyfard could not surprise her. She slipped her hand into her pocket and took out the toy. Deborah blinked; its feathers were now white, pure as goose down, or clouds. She thought back to the crypt. The bird had definitely been blue before. She remembered thinking it was the blue of a summer sky. Could she have been mistaken? Or was this some new aspect of the machinery?

Deborah felt strange; she was lightheaded and her hands tingled. She should hide the bird in her room, perhaps under her mattress. But when she tried to leave it behind, her fingers would not let it go. Just having the bird made Deborah feel more relaxed. Would it really matter if she left it in her pocket? She slipped the bird back in, unlocked the door, then lay down and closed her eyes.

About the Authors and their Work

ANGELA JAMESON

Angela Jameson showed a passion for stories and language at a young age, and after graduating from UCL in Dutch and History of Art, her career took her into translation and non-fiction writing in London and Amsterdam and then Cambridge. In 2017, Angela completed an MA in Creative Writing at ARU. Her debut novel, *Against The Tide*, is inspired by the true accounts of women on the north-east coast of England, who supported their communities' independent lifeboats prior to the arrival of the RNLI. You can find Angela as @jammyanj on Instagram and Threads.

Against the Tide

Against The Tide is a feminist coming-of-age story set against the dramatic backdrop of a 19th-century fishing community struggling to cope with the knock-on effects of the industrial revolution.

Maggie is the 16-year-old daughter of John Scott, fisherman and coxswain of the Whitby lifeboat. Her dreams of becoming a teacher are crushed when her family is struck by tragedy and her father tells Maggie to give up her training. Maggie becomes increasingly isolated in her new role and, after a lifeboat crewman dies during a straightforward rescue, she suspects her father is hiding something that could have prevented the accident. Not knowing where to turn, support comes from unexpected places, but Maggie decides to take matters into her own hands. Help cannot come soon enough to avert another disaster, however, and Maggie is forced into a desperate situation when a ferocious storm hits the Whitby coast.

The novel is fraught with struggle: class struggle on the part of the fishermen who fear for their livelihoods if the RNLI take on their lifeboat work; the fisherwomen's struggle for emancipation, and the struggle against the unpredictable forces of nature.

NORA KEREZOVIC

The love of storytelling and writing led Nora Kerezovic to study journalism in Dublin. Having worked as a reporter for newspapers in Ireland, she moved to London to work for ten years at BBC Worldwide as an Editor. When she and her husband started a family, Nora decided to freelance. She worked on educational material, prompting her to become an adult tutor. With that came a desire to work in social care. Since then, she has designed and delivered tailor-made engaging and empowering workshops on creative writing and wellbeing to vulnerable adults, people with learning disabilities, mental health needs, and survivors of human trafficking. You can find Nora on Instagram @onthewritepath.

Under your Eyes

Cecelia Kennedy is overwhelmed. She feels shackled to the grief of losing her father and the post-natal depression that follows the birth of her first born, Daniel. Returning to work, as a creative director for a

London-based cosmetics company, brings both joy and challenges. Her husband, Stuart, an award-winning news editor sifts through lies and facts for a living. He has made enemies and there's one, right under his eyes, who is closely watching Cecelia. And waiting...

When Cecelia storms off at the airport after an argument, Stuart takes their scheduled flight to Dublin, with Daniel, convinced that Cecelia will take a separate flight. Why would she miss her niece's christening when she's the Godmother? But Cecelia doesn't make it to Dublin.

Drugged and disillusioned, she discovers she's in the home of Harry, Stuart's employee, deep in the heart of Sussex, surrounded by miles of forest, isolation and silence. Harry believes Stuart is a tyrant and says he wants to save Cecelia. She soon learns that the only way for her to escape is through her captor's dark mind.

TALISHA MCKNIGHT (TATIANA HANDFIELD)

Tatiana Handfield (writing as Talisha McKnight) is a trained Secondary School teacher of English Language and Literature. She enjoys writing short stories, poems, plays and children's books which display and celebrate the vibrantly unique culture of her home country the Turks and Caicos Islands. Tatiana is the founder and creative director of Cyril & Dorsie Publishing, which focuses on publishing literature centred on the history, culture and heritage of the Turks & Caicos. You can follow Tatiana on Instagram and Threads: @tanishahandfield.

When You See Me I'm Gone

Sometimes missing things aren't always lost, they're trapped and sometimes trapped things don't always need to be rescued, are the cryptic words uttered by Tanisha's grandmother following her parents' disappearance.

On the eve of her 17th birthday, Tanisha receives the eerie news of her parents' disappearance during a diving expedition. Catapulted early from her boarding school she is transported to Belle Isle, the small island where her parents grew up, to reside with her grandparents. Six months later her parents are declared dead, but Tanisha isn't convinced of this verdict. Prompted by her suspicions, she begins investigating strange happenings around the small island, a mysterious investment group and a glowing presence near the reef.

GAVIN MARSHALL

For the last 35 years Gavin Marshall has been involved in telling stories as a trapeze artist, actor and director. His work has included shows for the Royal Shakespeare Company, circus spectacles in Macau, India and the UAE, roles in the West End and Bollywood epics, as well as motion capture for Andy Serkis and Spielberg movies. Having loved every minute of telling other people's stories, he is finally telling his own.

The Boy Who Fell is an extract from the novel *The Sea of Ghosts*

When Dani's stepbrother Matthew is sucked through his hospital bed into a strangerous land full of talking beasts, quarrelling pirates and tyrannical fire demons, she must follow to rescue him.

Here in the Birl, lost souls' memories fall as star pearls to dissolve in a Sea of Ghosts or are snatched from the waters by pirates to be sold to the highest bidder. When Dani enlists the help of Lop Eyed Lil the pirate Queen, she suspects the old sea dog knows more than she is letting on. And when she finds her brother frozen in ice beneath the River City Palace, betrayed, it seems, by Lil herself, her worst fears are realised. But their only way home is through the Lighthouse beyond the Sea of Ghosts. And the only one who can help them get there… is Lil.

Stripped of his memories in this strange new world, can Matthew learn to trust himself? And embittered by her family's break-up, can Dani learn to trust others as she seeks to find their way home?

DAPHNE MAYS (CATHERINE OLIVER)

Catherine Oliver, 30 years old, also known by her pseudonym Daphne Mays, lives in Switzerland with her partner. She is a full-time night shift nurse in a care home and has been a nurse for over ten years. Catherine has always wanted to write a book about her experiences as a caregiver.

Geissberg

What is Geissberg? A hotel, a care home, or a living nightmare?

The ordinary life of a young mother, Anneli Beldi, turns to terror when she starts to hallucinate and hears a man's cry for help in the woods. As the mist blocks her view, she finds herself lost. Who will she meet, and will she find her way back out?

Stephanie Bolliger, a nurse in a care home for the elderly, uncovers a shocking truth through her Tibetan colleague, nurse-in-training, Michewa. The investors of the care home, it seems, have been perpetuating a lie to maintain control and profit from the suffering of the elderly. Nurse Stephanie and Michewa hatch a plan to help the elderly residents escape the clutches of the care home. Will they be able to execute their plan without arousing suspicion? Or will the corporate might of the retirement facility prove too great?

EMMA ROGERS

Emma Rogers lives on the (mostly) sunny south coast of England near Hastings, where she works in Adult Social Care. She writes: "Following a health scare three years ago, I know what it feels like to be given a "wake up call", and how it can lead to a reassessment of what's important in life.

The Four Loves of Professor Waldman

Every scar tells a story.

Waldman, Professor of Anatomy, is forced to confront his own mortality when he is the victim of a violent assault. When he wakes in hospital, Waldman finds his life fundamentally changed, and forges a strong bond with the nurse who cares for him.

His friendship with former student, Henry, strengthens and their roles reverse when Henry realises his mentor now needs mentoring. As Waldman learns how to navigate the road to recovery and rebuild his life, can he forgive the man responsible for causing him so much pain?

Ten years later, Waldman has fallen in love with Annie Schultze. When her safety is threatened, Waldman intervenes, unlocking a chain of events which sees him compelled to reveal the secret he has kept from his friends. Can his friendship with Henry and his fledgling love affair with Annie survive the revelation?

A contemporary story set in Ingolstadt, Germany, the novel features characters and the university setting from Mary Shelley's Frankenstein, and explores themes of trauma and forgiveness, love and friendship, rebirth and transformation.

FARHANA SHAIKH

Farhana Shaikh is a writer and publisher born in Leicester. She established Dahlia Books, a small press from the corner of her kitchen. Farhana won the Penguin/Travelex Next Great Travel Writer prize. She was longlisted for the Spread the Word Life Writing Prize for her memoir about growing up in 1980s Leicester. Her short play *Risk* was produced as part of Kali Theatre's discovery programme and staged at Curve Leicester. Her first novel, *No Place for a Young Woman* was longlisted in the Women's Prize/CBC Creative #Discoveries2023. Farhana teaches marketing at De Montfort University and runs the Middle Way Mentoring project. Find her on X/Twitter @farhanashaikh.

No Place for a Young Woman – A reimagining of Pride and Prejudice set in 1960s India.

The Shahs have four daughters – Khadija, Ayesha, Maryam and Choti. Their mother, Zubeida is desperate to see them married before the dowry prohibition act is enforced and a new school for girls is built.

As the sisters work together to produce a quilt, they explore their individual identities and what they want out of life. Khadijah is happy to do what her family thinks is best. Fiercely independent, Ayesha would rather read books than entertain prospective husbands. She is adamant she will only marry on her own terms, if at all. Maryam considers the religious benefits, and Choti – who is obsessed by Bollywood – only wishes to be adored.

Set against the backdrop of a transforming India, with a female minister rising through the ranks and a thriving movie industry, the novel explores themes of tradition vs. modernity, family vs. individualism and love vs. duty. While the sisters all have their own dreams and ambitions, the novel follows Ayesha's story.

JACQUELINE SMITH

Jacqueline Smith studied Marine Biology at university and has been forever fascinated by the ocean. After conservation work abroad, she returned to the UK and trained to become a teacher, educating in schools and other settings including the Natural History Museum and Kew Gardens. She is drawn to writing that engages with nature and the environment and *Unholy Sea,* her first novel, was partly inspired by true events.

Unholy Sea

A young couple collide amidst the exuberance of New Year's Eve fireworks at Raffles, Singapore. The year is 1991. Together they embark on a journey through Java to Bali, with its seductive beauty and mysterious spirit worlds. Working as divers, they experience an underwater world of extraordinary beauty and unseen dangers, whilst on land they strive for acceptance into a complex culture.

But both are carrying secrets as they walk their tightrope of joie de vivre and tragedy together. Can their love survive the journey and is it ever really possible to leave the past behind?

Unholy Sea explores the naivety and vulnerability of youth, whilst celebrating the wonder and vitality of that stage of life which allows such adventures to happen. Ultimately there is tragedy, but the themes of healing and hope run through the story, both aided by the natural world encountered by the characters.

LINDA KAY STEVENS

Linda Kay Stevens was born in Utah and raised in a loving family who were perpetually on the move. Her diverse experiences span from the wilds of the Rocky Mountains to the shores of the Ionian Sea. She gathers and layers her writing with a quest to understand her six-plus decades of movement through prose and poetry.

Linda Kay divides her time between living in a meditation community in Suffolk, England and a secluded Greek forest on Corfu island, with her life partner.

They share the bounty with a dozen chickens, a couple of friendly feral cats, and two rescue hounds who love to accompany her on the trails. You can connect with Linda on Instagram @goldenphoenixwoman.

Eve

Drawn from a larger work entitled *Brother Moon*, *Eve* explores sexuality in relation to Mother-Daughter lineage. In her work, Linda Kay creates a memoir map consisting of poetic fragments that seek to illuminate the experience of sexual blossoming, waxing side by side with her brother whose adolescence waned in the shadow of muscular dystrophy.

Dreamscapes, mother-daughter dialogues, and memories enhanced by shamanic experiences and plant ceremonies capture glimpses of her experience.

Stories of the all-American family road trip and extensive moving about – seeking, always searching for home, showcase the characters' resilience in the face of adversity. Collectively, these stories tell the tale of a girl whose unfolding from childhood through adolescence onward to adulthood culminates in her becoming a crone-woman living the life of an expatriate in Corfu, Greece.

GEORGE WALLACE

George Wallace has been writing for two years. He is a chartered engineer and has been employed in aircraft design, air traffic control design, and the maritime industry. A keen race walker, he recently came first in

Walk the Walk, covering 15.2 miles in 3.5 hours.

The Death Spell of Solari

Deborah, chief embalmer of the crypt in Solari Castle, has the power of Ocjilif (magic) but does not know it. Solari Castle has a spell on it and during the embalming of the Queen Mother, Deborah is caught using Ocjilif. Sentenced to death, she escapes with a task of finding the missing prince, who has been gone for five years.

Deborah finds the prince, all the while her powers of Ocjilif growing. When the prince gets into trouble at the castle, he calls on Deborah to help him out. There, Deborah and her team find the missing spell and create the potion to set the Castle and its occupants free at last.

To contact our writers:

If you are an agent or publisher who wishes to see a full manuscript or discuss representation of one of our writers, please contact them via The Writing Coach.

You can email: jacqui@thewritingcoach.co.uk

About The Writing Coach

The Writing Coach was founded in 2005 by the novelist Jacqui Lofthouse. An international mentoring and development organization, we are also an online home for writers – somewhere you can find advice, information, motivation and, most of all, encouragement for your writing work.

We help writers to develop confidence, craft and industry connections through coaching, community and retreats so that they can get published and share their important stories with the world. We also submit work to literary agents on behalf of our coaching clients. Behind all that we do is a desire to truly support writers – to enable them to create fulfilling, successful and sustainable writing lives.

Email us at: jacqui@thewritingcoach.co.uk
Our website: www.thewritingcoach.co.uk

Follow us on Facebook and Instagram:
www.facebook.com/writingcoachuk
www.instagram.com/thewritingcoach

Join our Facebook Community:
www.facebook.com/groups/yourliterarycommunity

Jacqui Lofthouse

Jacqui Lofthouse is the author of four novels, *The Temple of Hymen* (Hamish Hamilton/Penguin 1995/1996), *Bluethroat Morning* (Bloomsbury 2000/Blackbird 2018), *Een Stille Verdwijning*, (De Bezige Bij 2005) and *The Modigliani Girl* (Blackbird 2015). Her novels have sold over 100,000 copies in the UK, the USA and Europe and have been widely reviewed.

'Deceptive; entertaining and unusual' – Louis de Bernières

'A thriller full of twists and turns that keeps the reader guessing. Every word is magical, almost luminous' – Daily Mail

'A very impressive book… a superbly recreated historical period and a passionate investigation into femininity, all wrapped up in a mysterious and well-paced narrative.' – Jonathan Coe

Also published by Nightingale Editions

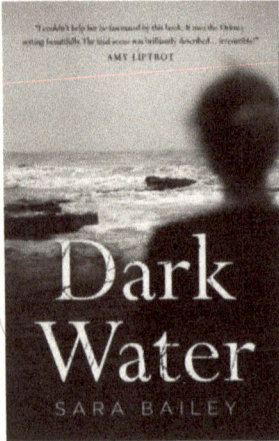

Dark Water
by Sara Bailey
www.orkneywriter.com

A psychologically intense portrait of adolescent yearning and obsession, set in the beautiful Orkney Islands.

Dr Sara Bailey is a writer, consultant and lecturer who has been working with authors and screenwriters for many years, in Richmond-upon-Thames, Winchester and Southampton. She has a PhD in Creative and Critical Writing from Bangor University. She lives in Orkney, the setting of her debut novel, Dark Water.

'I couldn't help but be fascinated by this book. It uses the Orkney setting beautifully. The final scene was brilliantly described... irresistible!' – Amy Liptrot

Acknowledgements

It has been my pleasure and privilege to work with our ten talented writers on this anthology. I'm so proud of what they have all achieved.

At The Writing Coach, I am lucky to have such a wonderful team: Jacqueline Smith; Emma Coxon and Andrea Callan. Our editors Julie-Ann Corrigan, Bryony Pearce, Nikki Sheehan and Heidi Williamson gave the writers excellent feedback on initial drafts. Rosalie Love was our superb copy editor.

My sincere thanks to Stephanie Zia, Founder of Blackbird Books, our formatter and publishing advisor. Nightingale Editions is an imprint of Blackbird, so Stephanie plays a vital role in the life of this book. The stunning cover was crafted by Charlotte Mouncey from Bookstyle. Thanks also to Zuaira Islam at Clays. I am grateful to our ten literary agents for their important contributions to this project.

A huge thank-you must also go to my family, David, Jack and Saskia who are always so incredibly supportive of my work at The Writing Coach. Without your encouragement and love, this book would not exist.

Jacqui Lofthouse, September 2024